Snarky in the Suburbs
Back to School

This is a work of fiction. All of the characters, organizations, and events portrayed in this novel are either products of the author's imagination or are used fictitiously.

For information contact Snarky at snarkyinthesuburbs@gmail.com or www.snarkyinthesuburbs.com

Many thanks to **"Team Snarky"** who helped turn my ramblings into a book.

Abby Ray, Rose McCord, Ann Owen, Peggy Hoogs, Angela M. Krout, Lisa Chase, Mary Endersbe, Brenda Marion, Lucy Carrion-Barnes, Elizabeth Foley, Megan Anzalone, Bonnie Lovitt, Heather Mayfield, Debbie Ackerman, Pam Winbolt Denise Newton, Dixie Crane, Leanne Schraeder, Karla S. Robinson, Susan Coulby, Lia Carson, Lorri White, Jennifer Holbert, Luwanna Cook, Emily Cerny, Julie Jakobi Rahbusch, Jane Owen, Angela Massey, Betsy Coffey, Brenda Marion, PM Greene, Beth Anderson, Holly Zimmerman, Katherine Morris, Lorri White, Simone Weissman, Donna Tice, Janice Simon, Jill Fitzpatrick, Denise Pickhinke,Tracy Jensen May, Christy Hogerty, Rose Sutkowski & Laura Fulton.

For anyone who has ever walked into a PTA
meeting and said "Holy Crap!"

New School Year's Eve

The real "new year" for any mother is not January first, but the day school starts. This is when we have our rebirth. We make goals and to-do lists and attempt to implement new and improved habits and routines like an actual bedtime for our children. Today is my New Year's Eve. It's the day before school starts and it's being kicked off with the annual Spring Creek Elementary School PTA Parent Coffee. Don't be mislead by the "Parent Coffee" label. No self-respecting dad has ever shown up for it. This is a pity because the coffee is a harbinger of all the delicious drama the new school year holds. I'm a woman who relishes drama. To me, drama is the buttercream frosting of life. Sure, you could live without it, but who would want to? Oh, I know it's unseemly to admit you enjoy drama, but drama is so much more than the overblown theatrics of attention-seeking females. Mom drama tells a story. By closely watching the nuances, you can learn so much from who's possibly cheating on their husband to which mom is making a calculated move to climb the ladder of the PTA hierarchy. All of this information is invaluable, especially to someone like me. I find it impossible to mind my own business. You may call this an immense character flaw. I call it the makings of a great humanitarian. Hi, I'm Wynn Butler, wife, mother and professional pot stirrer.

If you think pot stirring is a bad thing, you could not be more wrong. I only stir the pot of people who, quite frankly, need their icky pot stirred. I'd like to think I've taken this skill to a new almost super hero-ish level. I'm a mom with cellulite and spider veins that resemble the Mississippi River on a Rand McNally map of the 48 contiguous states, fighting for truth, justice and revenge (including, but not limited to, schemes, pay back scenarios and much-needed comeuppances).

5

I believe I've always had this talent seared into my genetic code, but I didn't reach my full pot stirring potential until I became a mother. Blame it on the estrogen surge, but you know how before you had kids you would take people's crap more? I did. I would suck it up, tell myself to let it go and move on. Motherhood (and maybe middle-age) changes that. It's one thing for someone to be mean spirited to you. It's another thing all together for that same person to exact their character flaw on your child (or really any children). I'm all about prevention - not letting this kind of thing happen, and if that doesn't work I move on to my specialty, remediation: the act of correcting an error, a fault or an evil. The PTA Coffee screams - remediate!

The coffee typically is held at a house inhabited by a family in the higher socioeconomic strata of the school district. This year, Jacardia (Jeh-car-de-ah) Monroe, my arch nemesis, is the hostess. Jacardia resembles an upside down broom, with the face of a really not-aging-well Taylor Swift and hair that would put Goldilocks, Rapunzel or any Disney Princess to shame, (think excessively long blonde ringlets). She looks rather like one of those Dollar Store off-brand Barbie dolls left out in sun to cure, kind of like a strip of beef jerky, if you bleached it white and then tried to iron out the wrinkles. I can sum her up with one sentence: She's the sort of woman who still, two decades after leaving college, insists on putting a sorority sticker on her Range Rover. Every time I see her in her car, I want to roll down my window and yell "Move on! You were a Pi Phi pledge when Bush the First, was President. There is not a SAE formal in your future!" She's also number three on my list of moms I'd like to Botox in the jugular with an epidural needle.

My first problem with her is I know for damn sure her real name isn't Jacardia. That's because women who've blown out forty candles on a birthday

6

cake weren't given those names when they entered the world, head first with a firm forceps yank, in the early 1970's. Here's what fortyish year old women are called: Amy, Michelle, Laura, Kimberly. No mom in 1971 named her kid "Jacardia." To turn my hunch into solid fact last year I asked Aleexiah, Jacardia's eight-year-old daughter, what her mom's real name is. "You know," I said, "What does your grandmother call her?"

She quickly replied, "Oh, my nana calls my mom Janet."

Bingo!

My other problem with Janet/Jacardia is that she brings back repressed memories from junior high. No, I didn't go to school with her, but she represents everything I used to fear. Here's the deal: I'm a big girl. By that I mean I'm working a size 12 pant (on a good day), a size 11 shoe and my shoulders are just a little bit broader than my husband's. I'm okay with that. I mean really, who cares? We grow up. We go to college. We have careers, marriages and children. All that junior high angst is but a distant memory right? Hell no.

This is what happens. Your kids go to school, and it's like you've time traveled back a couple of decades. It's been eight years, but I remember my son's first day of kindergarten like it was an hour ago. There I was clutching his hand and feeling more vulnerable than I ever had in my entire life. I was about to voluntarily surrender him over to another woman. As I was fighting back tears I had my first Jacardia sighting. You could tell she was the lead dog in a pack of moms with perfectly blown out hair and breasts that in no way were in accordance with their body mass index yet defied gravity and quite possibly, the speed of light and sound as well. They were whisper dissing about the other kindergarten moms, and here's the good manner's deal breaker - the other kids. Who disses five-year-olds, except other five-year-olds? Certainly not other moms! My son Clay was getting dissed because of his haircut. The day before kindergarten he decided to give himself a trim. Suffice it say, based on what he did to his hair, I don't see a future for him in the beauty industry. I did get my stylist to do her best to fix it, but he was still sporting some very short hair, which, I thought, he was totally pulling off.

It was then I realized, as I was breaking out in a cold sweat, that I was surrounded by older versions of the girls who taunted me in junior high school. They weren't the same exact girls that terrorized me, but they were the same type. The posse of bitchy "Gee Your Hair Smells Terrific" females were back in my life as mothers and now they've weaponized - they've spawned. Creating smaller and possibly, but not always, more evil versions of themselves as ammunition. Right then and there is when I decided I had no choice, but to declare war on these toned armed, collagen enhanced, cliquey, cruel, haughty moms. It was one thing for me to endure (or worse hide from) these type of females in junior high, but now the stakes were so much higher. I had kids and no way was I going to let these women mess with mine or anyone else's children. It was time to stand strong.

It took me a while to work up the courage. At first, I tried the kill-them-with-kindness routine, which lasted till Christmas and was a disaster. All it did was make me their doormat. Then I went to Plan B - ignoring them which took me through spring break. After that, I mustered my courage and declared war.

You may be thinking a declaration of war is a little over the top or even that I should have tried more earnestly to make friends with the Hot Mom Herd. The problem with the whole friend thing is I'm so not HMH material. Primarily, because I don't have a Ph.D in Evil or hold dual positions on the PTA and HOA boards wielding power like Mrs. Darth Vadar on her period (which is a really, really bad thing because Mrs. Vadar's cycles are based on the Endor moon, which means every 14 days it's a go). Then there's the other stuff. I don't have the single-digit body mass index. My breasts are original to owner and aren't inflated, hoisted and cantilevered to the point of creating a book shelf for my chin. There is no closet in my house just for yoga pants and Uggs. Shopping isn't my avocation. I don't worship the holy trinity of acid based fillers - Restylane, Juvederm and Radiesse, and I've managed to steer clear of a vajazzle. I mean really, who would want one? Those crystal things would so snag your Spanx!

I know this sounds harsh, with bitter overtones, and is flavored with a smattering of jealousy. All things my mother told me were very unattractive qualities. I freely admit that I might be suffering from the smallest sliver of envy. I'm a mom who buys clothes in the double digits, suffers from a debilitating case of ankle calf hypertrophy (cankles) and my shirts are a nice and roomy L to XL. I wouldn't be human if I didn't harbor resentment to women who could wear things like skinny jeans, let alone something called "toothpick denim." I can't even wear corduroy pants because my thighs rub together so furiously when I walk that it sounds like someone is running a terry cloth towel over a cheese grater. Plus, with all that friction I'm afraid my pants might spontaneously combust! But, besides coveting their trim thighs I'm really, I swear, not that envious. I like that I'm okay with dropping my kids off at school without the benefit of concealer and lip plumping, high impact gloss. I have a lot to be grateful for. I'm in love (most days) with my husband Sam. He's the city

9

attorney and the boy next door all grown up. We started dating in high school and got married the day we both graduated from college. Genius move on my part. I know a good thing when I see it. Sam had everything I wanted in a man. He thinks I'm funny, *does not* think I have cankles, is kind and met my strict IQ demands. My genetic code needed a pretty significant upgrade. I had to marry a man with optimum brainpower who could help dilute the dumb ass gene that's been running rampant in my family for generations. No way did I want to pass that on to my kids. It's too soon to tell definitely, but I dare to dream that my thirteen-year-old son Clay and my eight-year-old daughter Grace will be dumb ass free.

Because I'm entering year eight of fighting the mean mom wars, I'm battle ready when I get to Jarcardia's big ass home after running the gated community gauntlet. By that I mean entering the damned security code four times before the protective portal to "The Land of the Second Mortgage" decides to slowly creak open. I'm so sick of these stupid coded entry gates that allegedly keep middle-class riff raff like me from entering freely. I told my two kids last month, "No more friends who live in gated neighborhoods. If I can't drive non-stop to your friend's house, then forget about it."

After I find a place to park (which is outside of the gates and requires me to leap over some impressive shrubbery that spells out the name of the subdivision) I re-apply my Lancome gift with purchase lipstick, notice my teeth look really yellow. (Damn you, Crest Whitestripes why don't you work?!) suck in my gut and got ready to see all of the Moms I hadn't missed, at all, all summer.

Now about this Mom Coffee - it's serious business. Oh sure, it's presented like it's a chance for everyone to be welcomed back into the warm embrace of the

PTA (Yeah, right.) and, as migraine inducing as it is, almost every mom attends out of sheer fear because if you don't, well, the chances are you'll be gossiped about with vigorous enthusiasm. I'm talking work schedules are shifted and babysitters are called in because it's a no kids allowed affair.

I'd like to say that I don't participate in the Mom Coffee game and show up in my "day pajamas" (Target track pants), a T-shirt, my brown (enhanced with sun kissed highlights) hair in a ponytail and tennis shoes. But, I was raised in the South, and an invitation demands that I put some effort into my appearance. I did the shower and groom and I'm walking up to Jacardia's 9,000 square foot (if you count the basement) French Chateau in my wide leg Gap pants, (An end of the season steal for just $12.00. I was so excited. My heart was racing as I pulled them over my thighs and wonder of wonder they fit and, wait for it - I didn't have to do the turbo gut suck in! You know, when you suck in your stomach so hard you get dizzy and start seeing spots.), my Ann Taylor Loft blouse and my Kohl's sandals (which I got with Kohl's cash - score!). The major faux pas with my outfit besides the fact that it proudly screams, "Clearance rack!" is that I'm entering the Mom Coffee without the must have, hot, fall designer handbag of the season. I don't worship on the altar of Gucci because the day I spend four figures on a purse is the day that my husband will dual schedule divorce proceedings and my competency hearing.

This means I enter the Mom Coffee totally purse-less (it's my way of saying "I surrender") with my car keys in my pants pocket adding a little extra thigh bulk I really don't need. I will share that I'm one of the only mothers who eat at the Mom Coffee. I walk in the door head straight for the dining room table and have myself a merry little carbfest. I'm just a girl who can't say "no" to coffee cake. After very adroitly piling a double-decker of baked goods on my plate and

11

politely stuffing my face I survey the room for friends. First though I have to say howdy to the hostess, Janet/Jacardia. She's not hard to find. All I need to do is look for that mass of blonde hair.

It takes me about three seconds to spot her and it's as if I've been blinded by a disco ball. Janet/Jacardia is wearing something called "Pixy Stix" skinny jeans with huge faux jewels adorning the back pockets. The jewels are so big that I'm afraid if she sits down they'll shred her couch upholstery. (Seriously, how does she drive a car in those pants?) Continuing with the bedazzled theme, Jacardia has on a glitter infused, shrunk-in-the-dryer tight, T-shirt with her terminal torpedo nipples looking like they're trying to drill their way through the earth's core. She's layered on probably a dozen David Yurman necklaces and is working some kind of Ugg platform wedge sandals that are so high, they're making her lean to the right.

"Janet," I say, (just to tick her off) "great turnout and this coffee cake is the bomb."

She corrects me with a drawn out sigh and says, "You know it's Jacardia and I wouldn't know about the coffee cake. I haven't had a carb since 2001."

Her loss, because the coffee cake is incredible. I take another bite and continue to make my version of small talk with Jacardia by inquiring about the woman she has answering her door wearing a black dress with a white, frilly apron.

"What's up with the maid costume?" I innocently inquire. "Did you get it from the Halloween Superstore that just opened up in the abandoned Walmart?"

12

She looks at me, attempts to frown, but is thwarted by her Botox, so she resorts to pouting her lips and says, in a bored, breathy voice, "Are you serious?"

I respond, "Well, I saw an outfit just like it there and thought maybe you were giving it a trial run before you wore it for trick-or-treat."

As I'm talking, I'm walking backwards to seek refuge at the dining room table with all the baked goods. I know she won't follow me. Jacardia is a diet vampire and being in a four foot proximity to carbohydrates is akin to throwing holy water on Dracula. Why all the somewhat sane mothers don't boycott this thing is beyond me. It's not like I haven't tried to organize a protest movement but, so far, no takers. It could be because the Mom Coffee is fairly decent entertainment. It's equal parts Show and Tell and Look What I Did This Summer. You've even got a little bit of Fashion Week for the suburban mom.

There's a handful of hotties who show up ready to walk that "Mom Runway." In this case, the runway is the path from the crystal-chandelier foyer to the marble-floor-cathedral-ceiling living room, to the faux French-Country-Sub-Zero-fridge-eight-burner-Viking-range kitchen. Once you arrive in the kitchen the "runway" loops through the lodge-inspired family room where the fashionista moms can strike a relaxed, yet pretentious final pose. Quite a few mothers get all Spanxed up for this event. I don't know about you, but I think wearing triple Spanx at 8:15 in the morning is a little distasteful.

The Mom Coffee is also where ladies entertain themselves by counting the summer plastic surgery procedures. It usually goes something like this: boob job, boob job, Botox, yikes, too much Botox, eye lift (Hmm, wasn't she a little

13

young for that?) Restylane, Restydon't and so on. Let's just say there are enough chemical fillers in Jacardia's living room that it probably qualifies for its own E.P.A. landfill designation. You also need sunglasses to protect your corneas from the glare of the recently-bleached teethed moms. Here's a safety tip: In case of an emergency, if you can't find a flashlight, grab one of these women. Their glow-in-the dark, UVA-emitting, L.E.D. light, teeth could serve as spotlights, creating landing beacons for first responders.

The highlight of the soiree is the purse parade. Anyone who has scored a designer handbag is all ready to show it off. Now, you know who has a new, thousand-dollar plus purse because they never set it down. The handbag stays securely gripped in their well-manicured hands or dangling off their shoulder. All the better for them to fondle with and for you to see.

Before I even make it back to the dining room for round two at the baked goods table, the PTA president Elizabeth, "Queen Liz," Derby, rings a sterling silver bell (of course) to quiet the crowd so she can say a few welcoming words. Liz, draped head to toe in that Burberry plaid stuff that looks like place mats from Pier One or a Catholic girls' school field hockey uniforms, suffers from an acute case of "Regal Fever." She seriously thinks she's descended from English royalty (Don't ever ask her about her family crest. You'll be time traveling back to William the Conqueror.) Her hobby is correcting other people's behavior.

Liz is a graduate of the National Academy of Protocol and Etiquette, which she believes has given her the right to tell you and your children that you're precariously close to being one lowly rung above white trash and really need to step it up. I, on numerous occasions, have pointed out to her it's atrocious etiquette to tell someone r-e-p-e-a-t-e-d-l-y they have bad manners, but she just

14

sticks her nose up in the air and walks away. Right when Queen Liz gets to the part where she begins hitting everybody up to donate to the Spring Creek PTA Education Fund someone shrieks, "It's a fake! A great big fake!" from the back of the living room.

I'm thinking, "Awesome!" The extra effort I took to apply lash booster before my mascara is now worth the grooming effort because I'll look fabulous while watching, what I'm hoping will be, a middle-aged chick fight. I follow the fracas and attempt to work my phone's video camera with one hand, while holding a slice of coffee cake with the other. Oh dear, alert Milan, one mom has accused another mom of trying to pass off a fake Prada as the real deal.

I quickly discover "Murchy" (Mom+Churchy) has started the argument. Murchy (real name Jen Weaver) has the distinction of having more plastic surgery than anyone I've known, and that's saying a lot because I lived in L.A. for three years. I don't think there's much left of her that is organic, from her reddish-gold hair extensions to dermal injections in her feet to give her more substantial toe cleavage. Murchy is one big artificial preservative, kind of like a Rice Krispy treat, if a Rice Krispy treat offered up a heaping, helping, of side boob. Of course, she won't admit to any of her procedures and offers up "living of life of faith" as the reason she looks so "fresh."

I don't care how many Bible study groups she chairs and organizes (which I'm sure focus more on the worshipping of recent advancements in cosmetic surgery then looking deep into the meaning of the Pauline Epistles), Murchy is a bully with a Bible. To prove my point, she is, right now, accusing the hardest working mother at Spring Creek Elementary, Kathy Ferguson, "Croc Mom," of passing off her purse as a Prada.

Kathy is known for two things. One is her love of Crocs. Spring, summer, winter and fall, she's always wearing a rubber shoe. She has a collection of fleece-lined Crocs for the colder months and I've seen her break out a gold Croc for more formal occasions. Her Croc fetish is superseded by her dedication to education and her ten-year-old triplets (two boys, one girl) who are scary smart. I know one of them will find the cure for cancer and the other two will probably colonize the rings of Saturn. I can see how Croc Mom carrying a Prada handbag has confused Murchy. The two don't really go together, but who cares. Murchy needs to chill out, but instead she's attacking Kathy.

"Your Crocs may be real, but that bag of yours is an *el fako*," Murchy announces. "Anyone can see it's lacking the characteristics of a true Prada bag. The logo plate is way too big and the leather, or should I say pleather, is so not designer."

Kathy is a lovely, sweet woman who has sacrificed herself on the altar of motherhood. By that I mean she does nothing for herself. All her effort is expended nurturing the brains of her exceptional children. Most days it doesn't even look like she's thoroughly brushed her hair, which is usually in a pony- tail with a circa-1980's scrunchie. I think the only makeup I've ever seen her wear is Burt's Bees Tinted Lip Balm. She's usually very timid so I'm surprised when she gently, but firmly replies, "My purse is vintage and I do believe the logo plates were bigger back in the day."

Murchy blurts out, "Vintage, as in outlet mall!"

Jacardia and Liz, step into the fray to try to restore some order to the meeting. Liz says she's an expert on Prada and volunteers to judge the authenticity of the

16

purse. She adjusts the Burberry headband on her black severe bob haircut and executes superior posture as she walks over to examine the purse. There's not a sound in the room. (Except for me eating the coffee cake I grabbed on my way to the throw down. I couldn't help myself. It has an incredible brown sugar crumble topping.) Liz takes the purse and begins her analysis. She's really getting into her verification duties, even going over the stitching inside the lining. Who knew Designer Handbag Authenticator was in the PTA President's job description?

I look away from the fashion C.S.I. team and see my very young, sweet, beautiful, teaches Pilates and has perhaps the best backside I've ever seen on a human being, got-knocked-up-at-19-and-is-25-with-a-son-in-first-grade friend, Nikki Sakowski across the room looking distressed. She looks at me and mouths, "Do something." Of course, I'm going to do something. I like Croc Mom, a lot and Murchy is number five on that epidural list I've already told you about. I nod my head at her, walk over and interrupt the handbag forensics, "Ah, excuse me," I say, "You can quit your quest for the handbag's origin of birth. I know for a fact the purse is a vintage Prada. It's from the 80's. You know big hair, big should pads, big Prada logo."

Jacardia looks over her shoulder at me and in a condescending voice asks, "How would you know what a vintage Prada purse looks like?"

"Well, of course," I say, "I'm no authority on designer leather goods, but my mother-in-law has one just like it and it's so valuable she's left it to my sister-in-law in her will."

The mother-in-law line is the perfect fib. If I had said my mother no one, taking one look at me, would believe that I had grown up in a household with a woman who took a Prada to the Piggly Wiggly. My mother-in-law on the other hand lives (thank you Higher Power) 2,000 miles away and no one has ever met her. It's conceivable that I could have married "above my station" and have a MIL who's a handbag connoisseur. In reality, her idea of high cotton is the Burlington Coat Factory and I totally love that about her. The genius is my line about leaving it to my sister-in-law. Everyone in the room can see my mother-in-law leaving me her vintage Tupperware, but a Prada, not so much.

I use my declaration of authenticity as a chance to reach in and yank the purse out of Queen Liz's clutches so I can give it back to Croc Mom. As I'm returning the handbag to its rightful owner I look at Murchy with her immense breasts (Seriously, they're so huge it looks like she must be lactating to feed quintuplets.) pushing out of her hot pink top and say, "What's wrong, jealous?"

Murchy sneers, "Not of you or her, e-v-e-r. Yuck."

Croc Mom quickly and quietly exits Jacardia's McMansion swinging her purse as she walks out. The good news is that the purse squabble broke up the meeting. As hard as Liz tries, no one wants to get "down to business." We're all spared the boring agenda and introduction of new PTA officers. Best of all, no one gets a chance to do the Education Fund shake down. There is one thing I did notice while finishing up the last of the pastries - something's up with Jacardia. There isn't anything specific I can point to, but I've got a bad feeling, and I don't think it's from eating half a coffee cake. Jacardia is acting extra full of herself, and she's seems sneaky, like she's planning something. This can't be good.

The Elementary School Open House

The Prada/Frada gossip is still going strong late in the afternoon as I get ready for the back-to-school eve rite of passage known as the elementary school open house. This meet your teacher shindig is held from 5 to 7 p.m. and besides having the kids check out their new classroom and even more importantly find out who's in their class, parents are also encouraged/coerced to volunteer for any number of "wonderful" opportunities. All hail the glory of the number two pencil, my oldest, Clay is in the eighth grade and has aged out of this ritual. As is my tradition, I have invited my closest mom friends over for a cocktail before the blessed event. Due to my superior skills with mixing libations I've created a signature beverage to celebrate the impending first day of school called the Happy Mama. It has peach vodka, peaches, lemon juice, simple sugar syrup and club soda. Total yumminess and with just enough alcohol to take the edge off, but not enough to cause you to loudly scream "shit" in the school hallway when you discover your child got the fifth grade teacher no one ever wants.

I'm sharing the story of the Prada/Frada with my trio of friends who are all congregated around my non-granite kitchen island. (You know you live in deep suburbia when you're judged by the geologic composite of your countertops. I've had six-year-old girls come to my house, look at my countertops and say in a disapproving tone, "Eww, this isn't granite." Who died and made freaking granite king?) My home is what real estate agents call the worst house in a nice neighborhood. Our yellow, two-story colonial is a terminal fixer upper that's recovering from being caught in the middle of an ugly custody battle. The house's previous owners fought over who would get to keep it in the divorce. The wife wanted to continue living in it, the husband wanted to sell it. The husband won so the wife did everything she could think of to reduce the value of

19

the home from removing all the bathroom fixtures to permanently scarring the wood floors with a crowbar. Her finest piece of destruction was ramming her Yukon Denali through the garage wall that goes into kitchen. Add in bad 1970's flocked wallpaper and you've got a house that was priced to sell. My husband and I have slowly been rehabilitating it. We're doing the dance known as the "Remodel Two-step." It goes something like this: Pay a contractor to do a project. Get mad that the project cost so much and vow to save money by doing the next project yourself. Begin a new project and realize (again) that you suck at home improvement and speed-dial the contractor. It wouldn't be so bad if my house wasn't an out-of-control diva. She's always demanding something from new electrical work to a paint job.

Sitting and sipping their Happy Mama's are gorgeous Nikki, with her six-year-old son Evan on her lap. She's helping me in the retelling of the Prada/Frada debacle. "Spreadsheet" Kelly Ruiz, a former IRS auditor and total kick ass in all things numerical, who is trying not to choke on her drink as she's laughing. Kelly is what I call a "mullet Mom." She works as a C.P.A. and because she's wound a little tight she never seems to be able to make the full switch from financial statements to mom duty or vice versa. For example, even when she has on crappy workout clothes her brown hair is business, bob perfection. Kelly and I are both still trying to lose our baby weight. It's been 96 months since our last child was born, but as I like to say, "It's a marathon not a sprint." My daughter Grace is best friends' with her twin eight-year-old girls Chloe and Sophia.

ABC, whom I consider my best friend, is rolling her eyeballs as I get going recounting my conversation with Jacardia. ABC is pretty and petite, with one of those short haircuts that not many women can pull off without looking butch.

She's also the only woman I know who's really a natural blonde. ABC's a mother to three very, how can I say this politely, turbo charged boys. We've been friends since our oldest kids were infants. We discovered each other in a breast-feeding support group. Of the ten mothers in the room we were the only ones not lying. While the rest of the moms were eloquently chirping about the wonders of natural childbirth, the joy of sleep deprivation, the musical, lilting sounds their babies make when they cry, and planting placenta trees, ABC and I were commiserating over how almost every orifice in our body had a sprung a leak. I even confessed that I had forsaken the overnight maxi for the multi-tasking Swiffer Wet Jet pad - much more absorbent and less chance of leakage. I even cut one in half and shoved a section into each cup of my nursing bra. ABC smiled at me, took her infant son's arm, gently lifted it up and said, "Baby Ben, wave at your Mommy's new best friend."

ABC's real name is Allison Inverness, but her good friends, with love, call her ABC because it stands for "Always Bitter Chick." You really can't blame ABC for being terminally ticked off. Her gorgeous dermatologist husband, the "Tri-State Restylane King," left her for a guy. Which, in a way, was a relief because according to ABC there were some major "performance issues." What sticks in her craw about the divorce wasn't the guy thing so much but the fact she wasted so many years torturing herself into physical perfection so she could get dumped for a dude. I'm determined to see ABC happy again. I'm currently very focused on getting her to taper off her boxed wine obsession. People are still talking about her behavior at the Homes Association's Annual Fourth-of-July parade when she took a carton of Franzia white wine, retrofitted the nozzle with a Silly Straw and then shoved it into a Babybjorn so she could drink and march in the parade. Her reasoning was it was a holiday and pretty freaking hot. I told her it was trademark worthy but gently suggested she may want to add a 12-Step program to her court mandated anger management classes.

As I pour everyone another round of Happy Mamas I ask Nikki, "Why do you think Murchy went off on Croc Mom like that?"

"Who knows? For someone who wears T-shirts that say, "Love, Hope, Joy & Jesus" and goes to like a million Bible studies a week she sure is vicious. I'm also positive she's batting less than 500 on the whole Ten Commandments of it all."

"Murchy is all talk and no walk on the Bible front, plus she's got an ulterior motive with her biblical studies," ABC eagerly shares.

"You're kidding," I say in mock disbelief, "she doesn't attend solely to repent for her sins?"

"Hardly. Murchy's got a sweet little 'shopportunity' business based on her New Testament study groups."

Kelly asks, "What does that mean?"

"It means that's where she sells her collection of cross necklaces, charm bracelets, earrings etc. I've been to one of her Bible studies and it's two percent prayer, five percent talking about the good book, thirty-three percent gossiping and sixty percent shopping. She's even got it set up as a nonprofit. Murchy says the money goes towards her charity."

"Really," I say, "She has a charity? What's it called, I Love Myself and Will Be Spending All This Money On New Cheek Implants?"

Kelly adds, "I hope she's being careful with the money or the IRS will be all over her. Do you think she realizes she has to actually use the money for charitable purposes?"

"Who knows, says Nikki. "I just wish she would go far, far away. I still have problems being around her. Y'all remember what she did to me last year, don't you?"

"Oh that," I say. "None of us will ever forget the prayer circle of doom."

The prayer circle is how Kelly, ABC and I all become fast friends with Nikki. Two weeks into the last school year Nikki was a fresh-faced, barely above-the-legal-drinking age, mom with her first child in kindergarten. New to the area, she had zero friends, so she was happy when Murchy invited her to attend the daily "Gathering of Moms." It's a group of women who meet thirty minutes before school gets out and hold group prayer in the Price Whacker parking lot, conveniently located down the street from the elementary school. (They used to do the prayer circle at the school but had to move due to that pesky separation of church and state thing.)

Nikki showed up for the gathering, excited to meet some other moms and hopefully make new friends when Murchy escorted her to where about fifteen cars were forming what looked like the 21st century version of circling the wagons. All the women, after parking their cars, as best they could, in circle mode, hopped out, then formed a human circle and held hands. Murchy pushed Nikki into the middle of the circle and began leading the moms in prayer for her immortal soul. Nikki, according to Murchy, committed the ultimate sin, (besides being younger and significantly more beautiful than any mom there) by allegedly having a child out of wedlock.

While this was all going down, I'm walking out of the Price Whacker after loading up on buy one, get one free rotisserie chickens. Usually, if I happen to hit the Price Whacker during the prayer circle time, I do my best to avoid it, but that day my car managed to be prayer circle adjacent. Yes, I believe in prayer, even prayer in parking lots. My issue with the "Gathering of Moms," is that I'm beyond over the breed of women who have managed to turn the four word phrase, "I'm praying for you" into a put down. They have perfected two different ways of saying it. One is "I'm praying for you because I'm better than you." Then there's "I'm praying for you because you have problems and I don't. Oh, happy day for me." These are just a couple of reasons why I avoid, at all cost, the "Gathering."

As I was putting my groceries in the back of my mini-van I heard someone crying. This caused me to poke my head in the circle. I was hoping Murchy was weeping because she had gotten a sign from the Lord, not to have a third tummy tuck. I quickly assessed the situation and it was not good. I marched into the middle of the circle, grabbed Nikki, who until that moment I had never seen before in my life, by the hand, and physically escorted her to the front seat of my car. She was sobbing, yet quickly told me what happened. I marched back to the circle and yelled, "You all suck! P.S. Her husband, not her baby daddy, but her husband, is serving in Afghanistan. She moved here to be closer to his family. So here's something you can do - pray for forgiveness and, I don't know, a functioning brain stem!"

I then turned and walked away, but I was still furious. The kind of furious where your whole body is shaking and your throat hurts from swallowing your anger so I went back and yelled, "And even if she did have a kid, or two or three before she was married, it's none of your damned business."

I didn't even notice that ABC was in the parking lot. Unbeknownst to me, she had gone to the Price Whacker for Capri Suns and Nutter Butters for her boys' after school snack. ABC walked up and shouted, "You're all a bunch of bitter crows and I know for a fact that three of your husbands' slept with mine! Go pray about that."

You can imagine how that went over - stunned silence and a couple of women looking really scared by that news flash. I glanced at ABC and mouthed "Really?" She smiled at me, shook her head and mouthed back, "NO" which made us both grin. I motioned to her to follow me to my car and there waiting for us was Kelly, also at the Price Whacker taking advantage of the awesome rotisserie chicken offer. She had the passenger door open to my minivan and was consoling Nikki.

"Kelly," I asked still beyond pissed, "did you see what just happened?"

"See it, no. Hear it, yes. I followed your, "You all suck" and it led me to Nikki. It is Nikki right?" She asked the young woman drying her eyes on her T-shirt in the front seat of my car.

"Yes, it's Nikki and thank you all so much. That was horrible."

"Don't worry about it," I told her. "Just forget those women."

"Yeah," said ABC. "They believe in the power of prayer, all right, the power for it to make them feel superior to others. Total bullshit. It's about time someone called them on it."

"But won't they hate you? I mean, will this hurt your friendship with the other moms?" Nikki timidly asked.

All three of us burst out laughing because the last thing we care about is whether or not any of those women like us. After that shared experience the four of us became tight. I'd like to think it was God's plan. I know, for sure, no one could have better friends.

As we all enjoy the last of our Happy Mamas I share my newest concern that Jacardia, sister wife of Satan, is up to something. Kelly, always the analytical one, asks for an example. I sigh and say, "I don't know, it's just a feeling I have. So everyone keep an eye on her."

"God, I hope her mini-me mean daughter Aleexiah is not in the twins' class this year," Kelly moans. "It should be school policy that your kid can't get stuck with her for two years in a row."

"Tell me about it," I said. "Grace has had to do three tours of duty with Aleexiah. Kindergarten, first, and second grade, and poor Clay has had Arabelleah in his class almost every year."

"It's not just Aleexiah, that's the killer," says ABC. "It's the combo platter of Aleexiah and Jarcardi that has teachers putting in for early retirement."

We all chug the last of our Happy Mamas. I pass around a tin of peppermint Altoids for booze-breath-be-gone, and then we corral our kids and each of us get in our own cars to head for the school. It's time to discover who has who in their class. I want to be one of the first in line when the doors open to the "award winning" Spring Creek Elementary. I have some Room Mom maneuvering to do.

Greeting the families at the entrance to the school is its mediocre leader, the principal, Mr. Parrish. Good God, he has on bike shorts. What the hell? As I get closer I hear him perkily announcing to everyone walking into the building how he rode his bike to the school's Open House because "Fitness Matters!" You know what else matters? Me keeping my visual acuity intact. Three years short of retirement, bald and pudgy Mr. Parrish is currently styling white, sweat soaked bike shorts. He might as well be wearing a translucent Speedo because it looks like Mr. Parrish has decided underwear is optional with his shorts. And what's up with the spandex of it all? Isn't it supposed to compress and suppress your bulgy bits? Because all I see, and believe me I'm trying to avert my eyes, is the principal's manhood evidently very happy that school is starting. As I use my body to shield my daughter from her principal's privates and hurry her down the hall towards the third grade classrooms, I'm thinking Mr. Parrish is acting very out of character. In all the years I've had a kid at Spring Creek, I don't think I've ever seen Mr. Parrish not wear a suit. Even on spirit T-shirt day he's got on pinstripes. My thought process is distracted by Grace.

"I can't believe I'm finally a third grader!" She says excitedly. "This means I'm no longer a baby. I'm almost half way through elementary school now."

"Oh, don't say that," I tell her. "It makes me sad. I don't want to think about you growing up.

"Don't worry Mom. I'm not going anywhere - yet!"

As if to assert her independence she lets go of my hand and saunters into her classroom all by herself, leaving me to walk in behind her. I smile as she introduces herself to her teacher, while I go over to the Room Mom sign-up sheet and happily write my name down.

I hope you're not asking, "What's the big deal about Room Mom?" Because all I have to say is get a pen and take notes, or at the very least highlight this information or trust me, you'll regret it later. Room Mom is so much more than just planning the parties, buying teacher gifts and organizing room volunteers. It's an all access, back stage pass to the teacher and therefore the school. As a Room Mom you can find out many useful things. My favorite, in no particular order, are: Teacher gossip, principal bashing, teacher not using names but subtly dissing other moms (love it!), inside scoop of upcoming activities, and sometimes if you're really lucky, the teacher will share intimate details of her life. This gives you the opportunity to transform your Room Mom status into Friend status. When this happens you've won the elementary school lottery. Your teacher/friend becomes your go to source for all things school related, not just when your child is in their class but for your whole elementary school Mom tenure. She's the person on the inside, your confidential informant.

Now, I try not to be greedy. I don't attempt to be the Room Mom every year. For example, last year I took a pass. Here's the most important part of my strategy - doing a ratio analysis that involves researching the teacher. This is

28

crucial. You need to find out what your input (time spent) and the teacher's output (information she will share with you) equals. If it's not close to being 60/40 it might not be worth your time. Next, I do a psychological profile and background check. If you have a teacher going through some personal issues (especially a divorce) - jackpot! You want to be her Room Mom. This is an excellent opportunity for a Room Mom to Friend conversion. Usually the success rates are very high. My research has shown the following teachers are good candidates for you to seek out the Room Mom position: Any teacher your age, any teacher with kids your kid's age (you already have a lot in common which could lead to a successful friend conversion), any first time teacher (they'll need your help and they'll be grateful), any older teacher (they've been around the block, aren't afraid to speak their mind due to job security and they usually enjoy sharing their knowledge of school politics). Teachers you *do not* want to be a Room Mom for: The male teachers. Don't even waste your time. They're clueless about any teacher break room dirt and are severely gossip challenged.

This school year, after doing my due diligence, I had decided I would be a perfect fit for Room Mom in my daughter's class. I had heard through the grapevine that her new teacher had recently gone through an ugly divorce and her only daughter had just left for college. This means her teacher could potentially be lonely and talkative. I was thinking I could make the Room Mom to Friend conversion happen by the Halloween party (which really would be unprecedented, usually it takes till at least the winter holiday party). I was fairly certain I would be the only mom to volunteer for the job until I discovered by looking at the name tags on the student's desks that my daughter had Coco Cutler in her class. Coca's an okay kid, but her mother Caroline Cutler is a manipulative, hot mess and for some reason is always Room Mom. She's also Jacardia's BFF. Talk about a demonic duo.

My dislike of Caroline begins with the fact she acts like she has the only functioning uterus west of the Mississippi. She walks around like she invented motherhood based solely on the fact that she's birthed a half-dozen kids. Caroline thinks of herself as the suburban equivalent of Angelina Jolie. In reality she looks more like a drag queen Cher impersonator I saw in Vegas two years ago. She has super long black hair, held back with those huge bug eye sunglasses and always, I mean always, wears black yoga pants and assorted Uggs with some variety of super tight T-shirt that I'm sure cost $300. Her claim to fame is not her brood, but the fact that she is a 00 (double zero). Not just any 00 mind you, but a 00 so tiny she's 000 (triple zero) adjacent as in, "I buy my True Religion jeans in the girls department at Nordstrom's."

Now, in the suburban landscape I inhabit, being a size 00 makes you the Queen. Everyone must bow down to your exquisite metabolism and your ability to subsist only on hot water with lemon and Listerine cinnamon breath strips. Caroline is so in love with her skeletal frame she travels with a Greek chorus. A group of moms that follow her around and hourly croon, "Oh my God, I can't believe you've had six kids and you're sooo skinny!" (Never mind she's had so many tummy tucks her belly button is almost as high as her boobs. I saw her in bikini last summer and her navel looked like a droopy third nipple.)

Caroline's favorite topic of conversation, besides her 19 inch waist, is dispensing child rearing advice, especially to parents whose kids offend her sense of size and proportion. God forbid, your son or daughter has a bit of a tummy or a little meat on their thighs because Caroline has no problem sharing

30

her weight reduction remedies. She professes to be writing a cookbook called, *The Skinny Family, A Mother of Six, Guide to Keeping Your Kids Thin*. I told her starving your children is usually not considered a recipe.

Her idea of parenting, like many mothers, is enrolling her children in as many activities as she can cram in one 24-hour period, thus reducing the amount of time she has to spend with her family. Her other specialty is foisting her kids off on the unsuspecting public. Let's take after school pick up as an example. Caroline will drive a two-seater car to school to retrieve four kids. This illustrates not a lack of math skills, but her clever, conniving mind. She'll immediately start her campaign of "Please Help Me."

It goes like this: "I just came from a meeting and didn't have time to go home and get the Escalade. Could anyone give my kids a quick ride home?"

Oh my, such a simple statement. Such an innocent request, but here's the problem - Caroline won't be home when you drive by her house to drop off one or most of her children. You'll call her on her cell phone. She doesn't answer. You end up taking her kids home with you for h-o-u-r-s. Finally, Caroline sends you a text and says, "I'm so sorry. I got hung up at (insert location of your choice) and didn't get your messages. I'll be right there." In Caroline speak "right there" can mean 30 minutes to 3 hours. Most, if not all, of the moms at school had been Carolined.

The thing, though, that really bites about Caroline is she thinks she's Super Mom. She signs up to volunteer for everything and does none of it well, if at all. A lot of times, she doesn't even show up.

Her excuse when you call her and ask "Hey, where are you this morning because you volunteered to work in the classroom today and you never made it in?" will be, "Oops, sorry I forget. I'm just incredibly busy."

Well, here's a tip - quit signing up for everything and showing up for nothing. Caroline's glory, the hope diamond in her "so busy" crown is always signing up to be the Room Mom in all four of her elementary school kids' classrooms. It's as if her highest achievement as a mother is seeing her name listed as Room Mom four times in the school directory. Never mind that she sucks at it and logistically you can't be in four places at once on party day. If you're Room Mom you need to stay in the classroom and run the party. Why the teachers ever select her to be Room Mom is a mystery.

As soon as I discover I'll be competing for Room Mom with Caroline, I quickly, dig out a hot pink Sharpie from my purse and write over my name on the sign sheet in big block letters. I then introduce myself to Grace's new teacher, Mrs. Nunez, and commence the back-to-school suck up routine. You know what I'm talking about - saying how excited I am for Grace to have her as a teacher, sharing how many wonderful things I heard about her, commenting on how cute the classroom looks, and then you always need to make a personal connection and remark on the teacher's shiny hair, cute shoes, or chic top.

Imagine my shock, an almost, "Are my eyes deceiving me?" moment, when after I have signed up for Room Mom and I'm in deep teacher chitchat that out of the corner of my eye, I see Caroline dressed in her uniform of black yoga pants, a fitted tee with Chanel C's all over it and fur lined Uggs (in late August, thank you) strut into the classroom with Jacardia outfitted in more denim bling wear. (Her jeans are so tight I'm sure they came with a 1-800-Yeast Infection number and a Monistat coupon.) Jacardia, whose daughter, praise God, isn't even in the class, distracts Mrs. Nunez by inserting herself and her hair into our conversation while Caroline picks up the Room Mom volunteer sheet and puts it in her freaking purse. NO!

I extricate myself from the teacher suck up and go over to my daughter Grace and whisper, "Did you just see that?"

Of course, she did. Grace, my brownish blonde haired child, who blessed be the wonders of DNA, did not inherit my cankles, but instead has her dad's slender frame, is probably the nosiest kid ever to walk the halls of Spring Creek Elementary; she also possesses freakishly long range hearing. It's really a little disturbing. When she was three I took her to an audiologist just to be sure she wasn't part barn owl. I swear Grace can hear a conversation from a mile away. She also suffers from acute curiosity. The worst thing you can tell her is not, "No you can't get another American Girl," but "Honey, that really is none of your business."

My nosey daughter whispers back, "Yes, Mom, I saw Mrs. Cutler take the sign-up sheet. Why do you think she did that?"

"I don't know," I answer, "but I don't like it. Do me a favor and go and find ABC, Nikki and Kelly."

"Okay Mom," she says, all excited to be a given a task. "I'll go get Nikki first because she's always the easiest to find. You just look where a bunch of dads are standing. Why do you think the dads always want to talk to Miss Nikki?"

Hmm, how to answer that question? You really don't want to tell you eight-year-old daughter the dads all congregate around Nikki because she's the hottest thing to hit their side of the cul-de-sac in years. With her lush, long brown hair, super model legs, pert, abundant boobs, big blue eyes and full lips, Nikki is organic Viagra. I'd hate her, really hate her, if she wasn't so damn nice and vulnerable. Nikki's like a baby bird that's fallen out of her nest. A beautiful baby bird, but helpless nevertheless. I see it as my job to make sure she survives this elementary school mom thing relatively unscathed.

I blow off Grace's question with a quick, "All the dads like her because she's so sweet. Now hurry, go round up ABC, Nikki and Kelly and bring them back to this classroom. Okay?"

"Got it, Mom," she says with a big smile on her face and a twinkle in her green eyes. She then takes off running. I can hear the sound of her flip-flops racing down the hall.

By this time Caroline has joined Jacardia in interrogating Mrs. Nunez. After asking if she ever pledged a sorority (gag) they both, almost in unison, beg to be her friend on Facebook. Say no, I'm praying, say no because if Mrs. Nunez says yes then I, not even day one into the school year, will lose complete respect for her.

I begin breathing again when Mrs. Nunez says, "Oh that sounds like fun, but I'm not on Facebook, such a shame."

Well played, Mrs. Nunez, well played. This teacher obviously knows her way around the pushy mom. After getting the Facebook cold shoulder, Jacardia hands the teacher what looks like a business card and says, "Well, you may not be on Facebook, but feel free to follow me on Twitter. Everyone tells me I'm inspirational. Here's my social media info."

Jacardia inspirational? Maybe in hell where she could be a life coach for Satan. I don't have time to ponder the long-term societal ramifications of Jacardia Monroe being a role model because I have to keep my eye on Caroline and that Room Mom sheet.

Luckily, it didn't take long for Grace to round up ABC, Kelly and Nikki. ABC looks intrigued. Kelly looks concerned and Nikki, as usual, looks gorgeously bewildered.

"Mom, Mom," Grace says. "Here they are. I was fast wasn't I?"

"You sure were honey. Way to go! Now, why don't you head to the cafeteria for the Ice Cream party with Chloe and Sofia and we'll meet you there in just a bit."

"Ice cream, yeah! See ya later." As the girls take off towards the cafeteria, I inform my BFF trio what I saw go down.

ABC whispers, "Damn Bitch," and then throws in a couple of F bombs. (I've never met anyone who delights in dropping F bombs more than ABC. She's even tried hypnosis and acupuncture to quit swearing, but it didn't take. The saving grace is that I've never heard ABC swear around anybody under 21. So that means Nikki just made the cut.)

While still keeping my eye on Caroline, who is currently talking Pilates with another mom that came into the classroom, I motion my friends into the hall so I can lay out my plan for getting back that sign-up sheet. It revolves around the enormous purse Caroline carts around. I swear it could do double duty as luggage or a laundry hamper. Lucky for me, her handbag doesn't have a zipper.

"Okay," I say, "Here's my strategy."

Before I can even get into the details Kelly says, "Just to be clear you actually saw Caroline take the sign-up sheet and cram it in her purse?"

"Kelly," get out of your IRS auditor mode. What are you going to do next, ask me for receipts for the past decade? Yes, that's exactly what I saw and I want that sheet back." I say in an exasperated whisper.

"Okay, calm down Drama Queen," she whispers back. "And just so you know under section 6501 A of the tax code the IRS is required to assess taxes within three years after your return was filed. So, there would be no need to go back 10 years for receipts."

I have to cut Kelly off. Once she gets started talking about the tax code she's hard to shut up.

"Kelly, Kelly," I say, "focus."

She comes out of her tax trace and says, "Oh sorry, what is it you want us to do?"

ABC answers that question with, "I think we should trip her or punch her. Yeah, let's punch her. She deserves a good punch."

God bless ABC, her separation and divorce triggered some serious anger management issues. She currently has three restraining orders filed, (unjustly, of course) against her. I don't think she would really hurt anyone. It's more a problem of her finding a proper outlet for self-expression. That, of course, doesn't stop me from whisper yelling, "Zip it, ABC! We're wasting time."

"Whatever, we're all ears so what's your plan?"

I quickly launch into the logistics, "Kelly, you and Nikki distract Caroline by asking her about her kids' soccer schedule."

You may be thinking this sounds lame, but trust me - it's not. It's the 21st century maternal conundrum of, "How in the world can I be at six soccer fields at the same time." It will be a total brain teaser for Caroline. A busy mom word problem: "If one mom has six kids and each child has two soccer games on the same day, three of the games at the same time, how long can the mom stay at each soccer game to make sure she sees all her kids play?"

"When the both of you have Caroline in deep thought," I continue, "I'm going to accidently, on purpose, walk into her making sure her handbag hits the floor. All three of us will quickly get down on the floor and help her pick up all her stuff. If, by chance, nothing spills out, the first one of us to hit the floor needs to dump the purse."

"What about me?" ABC says feeling left out, "What am I going to do?"

"You, ABC, are going to keep Caroline from picking up her purse. I need you, before she has a chance to even bend her knees, to rush in and ask her favorite question in the whole wide world, how does she stay so skinny?

37

"Oh perfect," says ABC with glee. "She can talk about that for hours."

"Yeah, and as she's talking, the rest of us will paw through her purse debris to find the sign-up sheet. Once I have it back in my possession and hidden, I'll take off and lay low until the end of the Open House and then return it to Mrs. Nunez. Once I'm out of sight ABC wraps up the skinny talk, then you two can give Caroline her purse back and it's mission accomplished. Any questions?"

"Nope," says Kelly, "But we better make our move right now. It looks like Caroline is leaving the classroom."

I look up and see Caroline walking towards the door, "Okay, okay," I say, "it's go time. Nikki, start the soccer talk."

Nikki seems nervous, but calls over to Caroline and says, "Hi there, gosh don't you look as pretty as ever."

Caroline grins, runs her fingers through her hair and says, "Girl, I was keeping my fingers crossed these 00 jeans fit. I seemed to have lost some weight this summer and was afraid they'd be falling off me."

Kelly chimes in with, "Hey, do you two know what the soccer schedule looks like this weekend? It sounds brutal. I think my girls have three games on Saturday?"

"Three games? Is that all? I wish my Saturday was going to be that easy. All six of mine have games this weekend and at last count that makes 12 games. 12 games and just one of me. I don't know how I'm going to do it."

That was my cue to walk right into Mrs. 00 and oh so subtly brush against her and delicately yank at her handbag. The whole delicately thing doesn't work so I resort to just grabbing it. That works. Down comes the purse to the floor and yes, the contents spill out right as I'm saying, "Oh my goodness I am so sorry. I'm such a klutz. Are you okay?"

A split second before Caroline bends down to pick up her purse, ABC gets in her face and says, "Caroline, how do you stay so skinny? When are you going to write that cookbook? You look so amazing, I don't even want to stand next to you."

Caroline straightens up, smiles again and launches with gusto into talking about her one true passion in life - herself. This keeps her busy and distracted while Nikki, Kelly and I pick up the contents of her purse and discover a surprise is waiting for us.

Instead of finding one Room Mom sign-up sheet we find four! Caroline had pilfered four separate Room Mom sheets. Kelly mouths, "crazy" and quickly hands them to me. I'm guessing Caroline goes into each of her kids' classrooms, removes the sign-up sheet and then returns it with her name on it. Out of the three sheets in my hand, one had already been messed with. I always thought Caroline was crossing out the Moms names and then writing her own, but she was smarter than I gave her credit for. She just squeezed her name on top of the first signature. I take the four sign-up sheets, stuff them in my handbag, and take off, leaving Kelly and Nikki to hand Caroline her purse and ABC to wrap up the "so skinny" conversation

The first thing I do, once I'm out of range of Caroline, is to return three of the sign-up sheets to their rightful classrooms. The one for my daughter's class I'm holding onto until the Open House is almost over. Then I'll take it back to Mrs. Nunez and tell her I had found it on the floor (which I had). Meanwhile, ABC, Kelly and Nikki are taking turns keeping an eye on Caroline while I lay low in the school library. My daughter keeps running back and forth with updates. Her most revealing report is, "Kelly says to tell you that Mrs. Cutler is looking, um, what's the word, oh yeah, flustered, very flustered and is attacking her purse trying to find the sheets."

Grace stops talking, takes a big breath and then asks, "Mom, why would Mrs. Cutler have bed sheets in her purse?"

"Grace, honey, she's not looking for bed sheets, but sheets of paper she lost. Don't worry about it and if you want some more ice cream, you better hurry back to the cafeteria. The Open House is about to be over. I'll meet you there in five minutes and then we'll go home."

"Okay, bye!"

I waste a couple of minutes looking at the *Dear America* books in the library and then with fingers crossed the Caroline coast is clear I return the Room Mom sign-up sheet to Mrs, Nunez and then make my way to the cafeteria.

I'm almost close enough to shout, "Grace, let's go!" when I feel a bony hand on my shoulder. I turn around and am greeted with, "Did you steal stuff out of my Kate Spade limited edition patent leather tote? I'm missing some important papers"

I give her a look that says, "Back off you unhinged estrogen pod with your belly button masquerading as a nipple," and reply, "of course I didn't steal from you. What kind of papers are you missing? If you can describe them, maybe I can help you find them."

Surprise, surprise, Caroline declines to offer a description.

I follow up with, "By any chance to do they look like Room Mom sign-up sheets?"

She glares at me. I glare back and add a lethal raised right eyebrow. I'm an excellent glarer so Caroline has no choice but to give up her glare and begin fidgeting with the 37 Pandora charms on her bracelet.

Then, I say, "I only asked about the sign-up sheets because I found some on the floor, four, to be exact and returned them to the teachers whose names were on them."

She shoots me an "I hate you" look as she sprints off so fast her yoga pants get stuck, just a little, in her butt crack. Too bad for her, she isn't fast enough to make it to four classrooms. As soon as she takes off, the principal gets on the P.A. system and announces the Open House is officially over. "Take that Caroline!" I say to myself. I'm almost giddy until I go to get Grace and see Jacardia watching me and smirking. The look on her frozen face is so creepy it gives me the chills. I leave the Open House thinking, "What in the hell is that woman up to?"

Sweet Dreams

Jacardia's smirking smile has me so freaked out I'm having trouble falling asleep. It's 1 a.m. and here I am smooshed in bed with two dogs, my snoring husband and an eight-year-old. That's right, my "I'll be a third-grader tomorrow" daughter, sleeps in the "marital bed". Not every night, but enough that I lie about it and make excuses to justify her habitual co-sleeping. My favorite fib I tell myself is that "I'm so amazing who would want to spend an entire night away from me?" That one, makes my husband laugh, a lot. My current rationale for letting her siesta in our bed is that tomorrow - well, as of right now today - is the first day of school and I wanted her to get a good night's sleep. I don't think I'll be dozing off anytime soon. I can't stop thinking about Jacardia. I keep telling myself I'm smarter than her and whatever she's up to I will figure it out. To boost my confidence I'm letting my mind wander back to what I consider my greatest elementary school Black Ops ever. When I successfully got the worst teacher in the history of Spring Creek Elementary, to flee the school in terror and never come back.

It happened four years ago, when my, now 13-year-old son, Clay was in the fourth grade. The alarm about the worst teacher ever began going off even before school began. It didn't help that this teacher was the only male educator at the school. Which lead some people in the administration to erroneously believe the complaining was unwarranted and brought on by over protective mamas that didn't want their kids to have a male teacher.

This was the teacher no one wanted, regardless of the gender. This teacher was a train wreck. A spiteful slacker. Imagine my surprise and horror on the day before school started when I found out that my son had received the school's "worst" teacher. Had I not volunteered for every fundraiser? Was I not on the PTA board? Had I not been the Room Mom the year before so I could suck up to his then teacher to make sure he didn't get this teacher? Did I not fill out the "teacher request" form where you couldn't name the teacher you wanted, but you could describe the "educational environment" that you felt was best for your child? And didn't my description of this "educational environment" point extremely enthusiastically away from this teacher? Yes, to all of the above.

My anger was volcanic. I marched right into the principal's office, unannounced, and said as I waved my son's teacher placement paper in the air, "Are you serious?"

Mr. Parrish, who likes to call himself "the voice of calm," which is code for "I don't like to rock the boat," looked at me, sighed and said, "What now?"

I gave him a look right back that has been known to cryogenically freeze a man's genitalia (at least that's what two former boyfriends and a former boss have told me) and said, "We've got a problem."

The principal tried to explain to me that some kids had to get "that" teacher and my son's former teachers thought he could "handle it just fine." I got the point that some kids did have to get "that" teacher. But why, did the school even have a teacher that no one wanted to "get"? That to me was the unacceptable part. I left his office, but not until he agreed that if after the first six weeks of the school year I felt that my son's educational growth was not being served adequately by "that'" teacher he would be moved into another class.

That evening, my husband Sam got to hear me moan and groan about what happened. His take is always a little different from mine. He's a city attorney so his brain thinks in building codes and lawsuits. He's also a big picture type of guy. My personality is to jump right in to any situation, but Sam thinks of the ripple effect and that's a very good thing because I've been known to cause a lot of ripples. Although, I like to think that my decision making process is based on facts. Back in the day I was a television news reporter (Never an anchor mind you due to chubby cheeks and lack of voluminous TV hair. I wanted to be a lawyer, but the stupid LSAT crushed that dream. Trust me on this one - every newsroom in the country is populated with people who bombed the LSAT.) and I pride myself on my data harvesting abilities. My husband claims that sometimes his common sense trumps my treasure trove of inside information. This was one of those instances.

Sam, looked up from his phone screen, took a sip of wine and said, "When we went to school our parents never changed our teachers. I don't think my parents even knew my teacher's name. Let it go. It could work out just fine."

Now, I know he does this in an attempt to talk me off the ledge, and yes, it does make me want to get off the ledge so I can strangle him. But, this time I had to take his advice. School started the next day and as far as Clay was concerned it was all "happy, happy, joy, joy".

Things did not begin well that first day. I walked into the fourth grade classroom with my son Clay. We were both loaded up with school supplies, and there is "that" teacher - Mr. Smithson. He's a middle-aged, pasty-faced goober with a receding hairline, a gut that looked like he was in the second trimester of a twin pregnancy and a toothpick in his mouth (not kidding), reclining all the way back is his chair, feet on his desk, wearing some athletic shorts and giving all who walk in an eyeball of dingy underwear.

This loser didn't possess the basic home training skills to be standing upright to meet his new students and parents. Parents were walking over to him, offering him their hand to shake and introducing themselves as he stayed reclined in his chair. Unbelievable. Then it dawned on me that he knew exactly what he was doing. It was a power play - an obvious and early "F-you" to the parents. I got my son settled at his desk and took some pencils to sharpen. It took an enormous amount of self-discipline not to accidentally on purpose kick his chair en route to the pencil sharpener so he would fall out of his "recliner." I also noticed that the classroom was not even decorated. It wasn't all back-to-school cute with bulletin boards with fall themes and the Presidents' heads on the wall it was plain Jane and a little stinky. Like it needed a couple of Febreze plug-ins. I took some pictures of my son at his desk and then it was time to leave. Oh, how I didn't want to leave my son in that room. I wanted to grab his still almost little hand and run out the door and begin home schooling. Okay, I can do this I told myself and I did have home schooling as my escape pod, so I patted my son on the back and walked out of the classroom.

Stories about Mr. Smithson began coming home every day. The other moms with kids in the class started sharing notes. It was the phone tree of despair. One month into the school year I had enough of all the phone calls and school pick up and drop off bitching and decided to host a meeting of concerned parents at my home one morning after school drop off. Mimosas would be served. At the top of my agenda was listing our "classroom issues." The list was lengthy and featured the central issue, that Mr. Smithson didn't teach. He put the kids in pods with worksheets for the day where they were encouraged to teach each other. He described it as "team building".

Meanwhile, Mr. Smithson sat at his desk playing video games on his laptop. His pod teaching method meant that our kids would come home every day with a stack of worksheets they didn't understand and couldn't finish in class. In essence all of us parents were homeschooling as we spent several hours each day after school teaching our children what was in the worksheets. It was like they had a ten hour school day. That's pretty long for a nine-year-old.

Even worse in my book was his method of dealing with the students. Mr. Smithson had a demeanor that was abusive. He was a bully. He would pick on the kids and give them nicknames. My son was "Geekatroid." He also called a chunky kid "Hungry" and a super skinny kid "Mr. Invisible." You get my point. Even worse, it led to all the kids calling each other these awful nicknames. It was all very *Lord of the Flies*. Add in his classroom control which was threatening and you had a fourth grade under siege.

Based on data, sweet-talked from the school secretary, (Always give the school office staff Barnes & Noble gift cards as Christmas and end of the year gifts. The return on investment is unprecedented.) Mr. Smithson's class had the highest absentee rate of students and his class had the highest percentage of kids that went to the nurses office with stomach and headaches. It was so bad that if my son called me from the nurse's office with the code phrase "extreme stomach cramps." I knew it meant he was having an awful day and I needed to come and rescue him - STAT.

We made our list and then decided Step 2 would be to have a conference with the school principal, present the list of grievances and demand some action be taken. This is where we had some drop off in participation. It's one thing to show up at someone's house and do the snack and bitch. It's another to sign

46

your name to a document and show up to a meeting. Out of the fourteen moms in attendance only six would sign the grievance list and only three of us volunteered go have a meeting with the principal. And I knew that at least one of the fourteen moms currently enjoying my hospitality would go pull a full Judas and betray us by tattling to Mr. Smithson by the end of the day. I adjourned my meeting, called the principal and requested a sit down with him the next morning and then prepared to stake out my son's classroom to see which mom would be doing the Judas.

Thirty minutes before the bell rang I positioned myself in the library where I had a clear view of the door into my son's classroom. At exactly 2:57, three minutes before the bell rang I spied a mom walking into the classroom. I tip toed out of the library and there she was Katie Kirkpatrick or as I like to call her behind her back and once in very close auditory range - "Fakey Face."

Katie is a master of sucking up to everyone and then cataloging everything you say for use in her rumor mill of flagrant lies. You look at Katie and she's an over exfoliated, perky, high pony tail, Merry Sunshine in a "Life is Good" T-shirt and sensible jean capris with Converse peace sign sneakers. Her whole looks says, "I'm a walking smiley face." In reality she's a vile shrew disguised as one of the nicest Moms at school - an American Girl doll gone rogue.

You know her type, she's all care and concern. Always volunteering to chair the hospitality committee for the PTA, and the first one at your door with a King Ranch casserole if you so much as had a cavity filled. It all sounds good right? But beware of hyper cheerful mom's bearing casseroles with Veleveeta cheese or low sodium Campbell's Cream of Mushroom soup. Her motive is seeking out information and then twisting it to suit her wicked ways. The big

47

problem is that only you and a couple of your close friends are on to her. Everyone else says, "On my God, she's sooo nice". Idiots. This means you can't openly bad mouth her because it would be like saying "Rainbows suck." "Puppies are gross" or "Panda Bears the Other White Meat."

That's a long way of saying I wasn't surprised in the least to see Fakey Face giving us up. I couldn't hear what she was saying, but I didn't' have too. I then saw Mr. Smithson jogging (or attempting to jog) to the principal's office to do, what I'm sure was, a preemptive strike on our meeting tomorrow.

The meeting with the principal went just like I thought it would. He politely listened to our concerns by nodding his head a couple of times, stroking his bald head and saying "hmmm", a lot. He took our list and said he would look into it immediately and then asked each of us to fill out a district complaint form regarding Mr. Smithson. I told the principal I would gladly fill out the form but doubted it would do any good, because I'm guessing his file probably has dozens of complaint forms in it already. I then cut to the chase and said, "What does it take to get rid of a teacher?"

Apparently, a lot. I got an earful about the educator dismissal procedure and it's a long drawn out process. What good is "No Child Left Behind", I ask you, if you can't leave a few teachers behind, as well? I know you might be thinking, "Girlfriend I would have gone into that meeting with a lawyer and threatened to sue the district."

Good point, but the whole attorney thing had been tried and nothing came of it. Yes, parents got their kids moved, but "that" teacher was still there. The two other moms and I left the meeting feeling like we had let our kids down and we were all on the fence about filling about the district complaint form. All three of us had younger kids working their way through the school. What if the teachers got ticked off that we filed a complaint against one of their coworkers? That's a big deal. Would they hold it against our kids? We didn't want our younger ones to suffer down the road. We all said goodbye and went home to lick our wounds.

Whenever I can't think I vacuum. As I was going back and forth over my wool family room rug that sheds worse than any dog I've ever owned (What's up with wool?) it came to me, a plan! We would get rid of this teacher and we would do it by dropping a "Mom Bomb" on his toothpick sucking self. I celebrated my genius by finishing off an entire sleeve of Chips Ahoy cookies. I had earned it. (Yes, I can eat that many cookies. It's one of my superpowers.)

After finishing the Chips Ahoy I got busy. I called the two moms that had gone to the principal's office with me and ABC even though she didn't even have a child in Mr. Smithson's class. I also contacted two moms who had kids in his class last year and were still eating bitter for breakfast over it. As we all know bitter is powerful fuel and I intended to throw a kerosene soaked match on it. In total, six moms were in and payback was just days away.

I laid out my "Mom Bomb" plan that next morning. After getting their kids to school my operatives reported to my house. Upon entering I had to call for a vow of silence. Nothing could be leaked. I also ratted out Fakey Face so the other moms could send laser beams of disgust her way. (I do so believe in sharing.) The plan, as I saw it, was perfect. The cleverness was in the simplicity. We were not going to do anything considered illegal in either civil or criminal court and it was very lady like, very mommish. We were going to stalk Mr. Smithson every hour of every school day.

49

Moms are experts at stalking. We've been stalked by our children since birth. How many of us have never had the pleasure of going to the bathroom by ourselves since having a child? Our school has an open door policy with parents. We are welcome to observe in any classroom and "observe" we would do. I had taken a notebook and wrote on it in very large print "Documentation." All of us would start out by taking a couple of hours during the week to sit in the back of his class and write down anything we wanted in the notebook. I didn't care if it was a grocery list. We just needed to look very busy and troubled as we wrote in the notebook. When another "volunteer" would come into the class we would make a big deal of handing off the notebook and doing some serious whisper action. Also in my stalkerazzi arsenal were the tools that said "good mommy, great school volunteer." I'm on the yearbook committee so my camera would be used to take pictures of him. Another mom did the school year-end video. We would set up her video camera just to tick him off and record his class. We also would use the P.E. volunteer stop watch to obnoxiously time his student interaction and then write it down dramatically in the documentation notebook.

Mr. Smithson would not even receive peace from us at lunch. The teacher's lounge and the workroom were combined so we would stalk him to the lounge and make copies of something during his lunch. The only way he could escape us is the restroom. But I had that covered too. The teacher restroom is the only adult size potty in the place so whenever we saw him going in we would stand outside the door, knock and politely ask, "Will you be done soon, Mr. Smithson?" Imagine the agony of having moms, who you know hate you, following you around every second of your work day. Surprisingly no one balked at the time commitment and we were ready to drop the "Mom Bomb" the next day.

I was the first one to begin the stalk-a-thon. I arrived with my son to class, plopped myself down in the sole adult chair in the back of the room and made a big deal about getting out my notebook. Mr. Smithson immediately came over to me and asked "What are you doing?"

I looked at him all innocent and said in my best "Go Team" cheerleader voice, "Just observing."

Oh, okay," he said, "for how long?"

"Golly, I don't know, I don't have much going on today I thought I just might spend the day here. I'll see how I feel after lunch."

He snorted at me. It was once of those man snorts that say, "We'll see about this." At lunch-time he went into the principal's office and tried to get me ousted. The principal came up to me and asked to "have a word."

"By all means," I replied smiling and then followed up with a "Goodness gracious" after the principal wanted to know what I was up to.

"Does it or does it not explicitly state in the school handbook, that you, yourself, wrote, that parents are allowed to observe in the classrooms at all times, expect during state testing. That, in fact, all we need to do is sign in at the front desk and get our visitor badge. Well, I've got my badge and I'm not leaving."

I then excused myself and started making copies in the lounge/workroom as Mr. Smithson ate his lunch. After five minutes he ducked into the bathroom where I, 20 seconds later, knocked on the door and asked how much longer did he think he would be in there.

Mr. Smithson spent all week trying to shake the six of us. He complained some more to the principal, had a temper tantrum about the video camera, the still camera and the stopwatch. We went all "Mom" on the principal.

"Wow, we're just taking pictures for the yearbook and so sorry about the video camera, but we have to have footage for the year-end video, and as for the stop watch we're using it to help time those multiplication tests."

Mr. Smithson continued his episodes of unhappiness. He had a fit about the three Moms "observing" who didn't even have kids in the class. Once again, I had to throw the principal's volunteer handbook back in his face when he confronted me about it.

"It never says anywhere in the handbook that you can only observe in a class you have children in. Therefore I believe all the mothers are within their rights to be in Mr. Smithson's classroom."

The teacher also tried to give us volunteer tasks to get us of out the room. Our response, "Um, no thank you. I'm fine sitting here."

I'm sure it was killing him that he had to put up his lap top and attempt to interact with his students. I even got him busted for bringing a non-district approved computer to the school. I was all, "Oh my, what if the students got a hold of it that would be real shame and what good are rules if the teacher, the role model, doesn't follow them."

Mr. Smithson turned out to be a great, big, colicky baby. One of those men that can dish it out to eight and nine-year-olds, but can't take it when it's handed right back to him. By week two he started sweating profusely and got the shakes. By week three he started taking sick days. By week five he had depleted all his sick and personal days. By week six he was on extended personal leave. By week eight we had a full-time substitute. Mrs. Brook was a wonderful teacher who was excited about finishing the school year with "such an awesome group of fourth graders." The next school year Mr. Smithson had transferred to a desk job in the administration building. Hopefully, he will never darken the door of a classroom again. We have Intel on him, just in case. To date his lazy butt has been sitting in a cubicle in a windowless district office for almost four years. I consider getting him away from teaching children one of my proudest accomplishments. If the PTA had any sense they would erect an obelisk (to resemble a sleeve of Chips Ahoy) in my honor at the entrance to the elementary school.

Reliving my moment of glory has had the desired effect. I'm now, finally, very sleepy.

Week Two of the School Year

The PTA Meeting

The first day of school went well for both my kids. My 8th grader even let me take a back-to-school picture. He was scowling, but I got my photo. It's now week two of the new school year and the call for parent involvement is in full swing. You may be wondering why I even bother to stay active in the elementary school. I know you're probably thinking anyone who can pull off such an impressive undertaking as getting a man to forsake his teaching career should be able to rest on their laurels and leave the heavy lifting to others. Sadly, that's not the case. Evil lurks among the Spring Creek school corridors and requires my constant vigilance.

I kid you not on this one. After my son started kindergarten I went back to work forty plus hours a week. This made me partially M.I.A. from doing face and volunteer time at the elementary school. After the economy went in the dumper I got laid off from my job at a marketing company. This allowed me to volunteer more at the school and you know what I discovered? In my three-year absence from attending a single PTA meeting, a cult of nefarious moms, led by Jacardia, had totally taken over. How did the other moms let that happen? I'm still busy trying to restore order.

Here's what I have learned the hard way. The elementary school mom game is high-stakes. You have to play to win and that means volunteering your ass off. Why? Because at any suburban school that proudly waves an exemplary, high achieving, or blue ribbon banner it's the moms who run it. Not the principal. Not the teachers. The moms who camp out at the school and do all

54

the behind-the-scenes maneuvering are the ones who make the rules. So, if you want to ensure that your children don't get the leftovers you hustle your yoga pant ass up there right now. You need to know how the sausage is made, especially if they're making it with your children.

Don't believe me? Think I'm exaggerating? (No worries, that happens a lot.) Have you ever wondered how three or four incredibly average kids, without fail, seem to get the most attention - the speaking parts in school plays, the inflated grades, always are the recipients of the benefit of the doubt or the eternal "do-over," never have to do any sick day make-up work and have so many *Student of the Month* certificates that you could wallpaper a downstairs half bath. It's all because they have a mother whose second home is the elementary school. She's up there advocating seven plus hours a day, five days a week, for her kids. It also didn't hurt that she gave the pregnant kindergarten teacher a Coach Diaper Bag as a gift. (FYI - it was from the Coach outlet. If those kind of things matter to you.)

The primary way to stay informed is by attending the monthly PTA meeting. Which is why at 8:15 this early fall morning, exactly eight days into the new school year, I'm perched on a way too small for my butt seat in the cafetorium, being tortured. One cheek is all that's fitting on the seat. I keep on shifting cheeks. It's like a mat Pilates workout- right cheek up, hold for five, relax, now left cheek up, repeat. Behold, in front of me on the stage is the PTA board lead by Queen Liz, with Jacardia as vice president, Katie Kirkpatrick as recording secretary, Caroline Cutler as membership director, Murchy as fundraising chair, who has a collection of large cross necklaces nestled in her cleavage zone to such an extent they look like they're nursing, and Kelly as treasurer.

55

It's like a "What's wrong with this picture?" to see lovely, classy, Kelly sitting on the stage with the cast of *Legally Blonde - The Perimenopausal Years*. Also joining them on the stage is the principal Mr. Parrish, thankfully he's not in bike shorts.

Liz begins the meeting by welcoming all the parents while she's caressing the ultimate Hot Mom accessory - the sacred PTA gavel. This, thanks to Jarcardi, has been bedazzled in crystals. After Liz's enthusiastic and yet bitchy welcome, Murchy stands up and begins the monthly back-to-school fundraising shakedown. Since it's September that means Gift Wrap & Cookie Dough.

The only thing keeping me from dozing off is my butt cheek work out where I've added a kegel squeeze, just to keep it interesting. I will give Murchy some props. Her sales presentation rivals and perhaps exceeds any Time Share pitch I've had to endure. The goal is for all the families to become a cog in a wheel of a gigantic Ponzi scheme that somehow will result in new Smart Boards (again) for the entire school. It's always about Smart Boards or new playground equipment. After Murchy shuts up and sits down, Kelly gets up to give the Treasurer report and lo and behold the PTA is sitting on a truckload of money. One newbie parent raises her hand and asks the eternal question, "If the PTA has so much money in the bank, why are our kids still having to aggressively fundraise?

Kelly, always the diplomat, smiles and says, "I think that great question is best directed to our president and principal."

She sits down and Queen Liz, still stroking the gavel, says in a regal tone, "The Spring Creek Elementary PTA is all about having a rainy day fund. We never want to have to say no to the school staff wish list because we decided to forgo fundraising. That's soooo not Spring Creek."

The way she says the last sentence is enough to make the mom who asked the question lower her head in shame and melt back into her seat. What do you want to bet this will be the last time she attends a PTA meeting?

The real answer to the question is the PTA fundraises because that's what they know and that's what always has been done. It's also a bit of a pissing contest. The Spring Creek PTA is known for its fundraising prowess. Even realtors brag about it when showing homes in the area. "You want your kids to go to Spring Creek. Their amazing PTA raised $200,000 last year."

Next on the agenda is the principal. Mr. Parrish, stands up and clears his throat. He looks over at Jacardia, smiles and says, "I'm very happy to announce that I've created a new position this year for Spring Creek. It's the office of Principal/Parent Liaison. The Principal/Parent Liaison will act as a conduit in helping me more quickly address the concerns of parents. Now, when a parent has an issue or suggestion their first step will be to seek help from the Liaison. The Liaison will also take over the duties of overseeing Student of the Month, the School Honor Role and our Academic Champion program."

As Mr. Parrish is talking, I'm wondering if the district has hired an assistant principal to learn the ropes before Mr. Parrish hits retirement road. I lean over and whisper to ABC, who's sitting next to me, "Have you heard anything about the school getting an assistant principal?"

She whispers back, "No, and I don't think the district has the money plus Spring Creek has never had an assistant principal."

Mr. Parrish, drones on a couple more seconds. He stops talking and smiles again at Jacardia. This time his grin is so big it shows almost all of his butterscotch hued teeth that look like Ricola cough drops. He takes a deep breath and says, "I'm pleased to share that the person that has accepted this volunteer position is one of our school's most beloved parents. Everyone please put your hands together and give Jacardia Monroe a round of applause. She's Spring Creek's first Principle/Parent Liaison!

Holy crap! Every parent in the cafetorium is stunned. For at least three seconds no one is applauding except Liz, Caroline, Fakie Face and Murchy. I look up on the stage and give Kelly a "What the hell" look. She gives me back the "I'm just as shocked as you are" shrug. ABC keeps elbowing me in the ribs. God, I wish she would stop doing that all the time. I don't care how many fat layers I have. It still hurts.

Jacardia stands up, heaves her hair over one shoulder and sashays to the principal. She gives him a hug and says, "I just want all of you to know that I'm so honored to be given this opportunity. When Ed, I mean Mr. Parrish, asked me to help the school in this way, I just couldn't say no. Everyone knows how much Spring Creek means to me and my family."

She then, hand to God, goes into the splits and cheers, "Go Spring Creek!"

Jacardia, at age forty whatever, is extremely proud of the fact that once upon a time she was a University of Florida Gator Girl cheerleader and she can still drop into the splits on command. I've seen her straddle the grass at the soccer fields and do a crotch drop before the second grade musical. Her excuse was a dad "had dared her." Another time, I was unlucky enough to behind Jacardia in

58

the grocery store checkout line when she was showing a handsome, young, cashier her gift of well-stretched hamstring and iliopsoas muscles.

After she closes her legs and gets off the floor, Jacardia licks her lips, and says, "So, remember if you need to talk to Mr. Parrish, talk to me first and I'll see if you really need to bother the principal with your problem. Chances are you don't. Oops, (giggles) I mean, chances are I'll be able to help."

The pissed off meter in the room is soaring. Parents began raising their hands and rattling off scenarios like, "So, you're telling me if I have a problem with my child's teacher I go to Jacardia? Is she like your appointment secretary or something?"

A mom whose kid has been an Academic Champion since kindergarten and lives to recite her son's report card and Lexile reading scores says, "Does this mean Jacardia will be selecting the Academic Champs all year? I see a problem with that already. Isn't that a job for the teachers?"

I might hop on over to team Jacardia if she can get rid of the Academic Champions group. It doesn't even make sense. Our kids don't get letter grades until fourth grade. So you're an academic champion if you get a S+ in circle time? All it does is cause the "My kid is a genius" parents to swarm and begin the *Festival of One Upping.* God help us all, the last time there was an Academic Champion presentation I had to endure over an hour of "My daughter not only reads one hour every night, but has also begun reading Japanese" (The dad failed to mention it was *Hello Kitty* comics with no words only pictures.) or "My son is already doing high school math is it okay to let him continue on with his algebraic equations or do we still really need to stick with those multiplication tables? I mean he knew those last year in kindergarten."

Ugh. If it were up to me, every parent would be told when their kid entered pre-school that their progeny was off the charts intelligent and better than any other placental mammal on earth. But in the interest of national security, the parents would need to keep this top secret and never share this classified information with the world at large. Can you imagine how the quality of your life would increase if you were spared from ever hearing the "my kid is smarter than your kid" boasting that starts post womb, picks up steam in elementary school then goes off the tracks straight into Bat Shit Crazyville right around the time of the S.A.T and Advanced Placement classes in high school? I have no doubt; we would all live in a much kinder and gentler world, if only this could happen.

As Academic Champ parents are getting feisty with Jacardia Mr. Parrish, begins mopping his sweating bald head with his shirt sleeve and tries to calm down the room. Jacardia seems to love the attention, hostilely answering questions. "Why no I'm not a secretary, never e-v-e-r! Why would there be a problem with me choosing the Academic Champs? It's grade school, not an Ivy."

While all this is going on I notice that ABC is staring at me. She finally asks, "Why aren't you doing anything? I feel a disturbance in the force Yoda."

"I'm just letting it all soak in," I say while watching Jacardia work the room. "Something's up, something bigger than Principal/Parent Liaison. That's what I'm going to focus on. Besides some parent will blow this whole thing out of the water in about two-seconds with FERPA. No, the bigger story is Jacardia and Mr. Parrish. Did you notice how she called him Ed? How he was smiling at her all goofy? And that hug? Who hugs the principal? Oh yeah, this is going to be good."

ABC looks at me like I'm crazy and says, "What the hell is FERPA and are you saying Jacardia and our school principal are getting it on?"

I smile and say, "I would say a slim 'maybe' on the getting it on. Although, I don't get the attraction, especially after seeing Mr. Parrish in bike shorts and FERPA is the Family Educational Rights and Privacy Act. Basically, it protects the privacy of student education records. Which means Mr. Parrish is full of it if he thinks he can let Jacardia anywhere near a kids G.P.A. or even their lunch money account."

"So, what's your plan? Don't sit there and pretend like you aren't conjuring up something? I've known you for more than ten years and I'm very familiar with that look in your eyes?"

Before I could even answer ABC, Kelly hurries over and says, "Why didn't you do anything? I was expecting you do something? This is all kinds of wrong."

"Calm down, I'm going to do something. I'm going to get up and congratulate Jacardia on her position."

"Why?" they both say in unison and then ABC says, "Besides, she'll know you're unbelievably insincere. You two hate each other."

"Because, ladies, I want Jacardia to think that she's won this round. I need to buy some time to do research."

"What kind of research?" ABC says getting ticked off. "She's an evil troll who will now try to get her manicured cloven hoofs on every kids records and do everything she can to gather information and use it to further her own agenda. Which as we all know is making sure her and her daughters Aleexiah and Arabelleah get everything they want. I think that's all the research you need Sherlock."

"Everything you just said is true, ABC, but I've got a hunch that there's a whole more going on and I know a way to find out."

"How?"

"I'm going to talk to my son."

"Really, that's your plan talking to your eighth grader?" says ABC.

"Yeah, because my eighth grader, Mr. Super Geek, recently converted a Roomba vacuum into a mobile surveillance drone."

"Okay, so not following you right now," she says.

"That means, ladies, that perhaps, I'll be gifting our principal, the anal neat freak, with his very own office Roomba. It could be the gift that keeps on giving."

Kelly sighs, looks at me and ABC, shakes her head and says, "This has arrest warrant written all over it."

The Mother & Son Conference

If there's one thing that drives me crazy it's a worrywart. You know what I'm talking about, people who turn worrying into a pastime or worse, a well-loved hobby. My motto, well one of many mottos, is "Worry less and do more." It's right behind, "You can never order too many Girl Scout Thin Mint cookies." Which is why at 4:00 p.m., a mere seven hours after the big Jacardia announcement, I'm in conference mode with my son, Clay, who is my doppelganger. He has my face, hair, and body build. Although, he is mercifully cankle-free. We're in the kitchen and I'm plying him with "Texas Tasty" cookies. These cookies have a little bit of everything in them: Oatmeal, chocolate chips, peanut butter, coconut and pecans. They're beyond delicious and my son loves them. As he keeps on sharing information with me about his Roomba turned surveillance drone, I give him another cookie.

You might think that using your kids for your own slightly nefarious deeds is, at the very least, unsound parenting, and at the very worst, illegal. This is where I play the Super Hero card. Think of everything Batman and Robin do. The dynamic-duo take the law into their own hands every day. Robin is the "boy wonder," which means he still falls under "minor child" status. So, if it's good enough for the Caped Crusader, it's surely good enough for me.

At thirteen, my son is what I would call a mega geek. This is the kid that for, the first decade of his life, my husband and I tried to find his "thing." We tried sports from soccer to fencing (yes fencing), art, theatre and music. Nothing was a good match. Then when he was ten, he hacked into our Bank of America account. We found out because he asked us, after seeing our meager bank balance, if we were poor. We said, "No, why do you ask?" That's when he got

63

his laptop and showed us how he got into our account and pointed to the balance. My husband looked at me a little freaked out and I said, "Well, I guess he's found his thing." Now, three years later, my son has what can best be described as a tech arsenal. I swear he could operate a nuclear sub from his room.

"Now sweetie," I ask, "does the Roomba vacuum and record what's happening in a room?"

"Mom," My son said, wiping the cookie crumbs off his face as he spoke, "You need to start listening better. The Roomba never worked. Remember? We got it from the 'broken bin' at Goodwill when I was looking for parts to harvest for the Robotic Club? Like you would ever pay that much money for a Roomba. They're $500.00."

Well, he was right about two things. I do need to start listening better and hell no on me ever paying that much for a vacuum unless it also unloads the dishwasher and folds laundry.

"Okay, okay," I said, "So, the Roomba doesn't vacuum, but you've rigged it to record voices?"

"Seriously, Mom record voices? What am I, a fourth grader? Manipulating its internal components and inserting a voice recorder is beginning robotics. What I did is install a camera with vocal recognition features that, on command, will send a live feed to my computer."

I gave him another cookie for that answer and continue, "Alright, let's say I took your jacked-up Roomba and put it in, I don't know, Mr. Parrish's office. Could you get it to send back what was happening to your computer?"

"Yes, I could program the live feed to start whenever Mr. Parrish started talking."

Now I had a moral dilemma. I didn't want to be spying on the principal 24/7. That would be *wrong-wrong*. I just wanted a teeny, tiny glimpse of what was going on in his office when he and Jacardia met behind closed doors. That would be not so wrong, right?

I asked my son, "What if I just wanted the Roomba to record, or live feed, whatever you call it, when it's two people in the same office. Could you program the Roomba to do that?"

He takes a swig of milk, puts his glass down and says, "Yes, but I'll need a sample of both people's voices so the computer can recognize them as its cue to start sending the feed. Oh, and Mom I'll need a clean recording of their voice, with little or no ambient sound."

"If I record their voices with my cell phone would that be good enough?" I ask.

"It would be iffy and it needs to be a good sample, not something with a bunch of traffic noise or kids screaming in the background."

"Could you use their phone greeting message or something like that?"

"Not really. I need a much longer sample to differentiate changes in a person's tone and pattern of speech."

"Okay, thanks honey," I say and kiss him on the forehead.

"Mom, you do know that it's illegal to record someone without their permission? You would be breaking federal and state laws, plus open yourself up to civil litigation as well."

Lord, what was he doing, reading the penal code in his downtime? I really need to get this kid to play outside more. Plus, now he's almost scared me straight. Notice I said almost.

"Of course I do, silly. I'm just curious, that's all, and for your educational benefit, I'm going to, maybe, get you those vocal samples and see if you can make it work. How fun would that be?"

"Not that fun, but I'll help you. Are we telling dad about this?"

"You don't need to worry about that. I'll keep your dad in the loop," I say as I hand him another cookie. (Keeping my husband "in the loop" means keeping him on a need to know basis. He can be a bit of a goodie two-shoes, pain in the butt.)

"Okay," my son says, "I'm in, but I'll need some supplies."

Which is his way of saying, "I'll do it, but it's going to cost you a trip to Best Buy." Now I have to figure out a way to get a clean recording of Jacardia's not-so-dulcet voice. I swear, I really don't know if I'm going to resort to even doing this. But right now, I don't have a better plan, so using my gift of being able to talk myself into doing something most people would run away from, I decide, to proceed full steam ahead until I come up with a worthier course of action.

The Favor

It was no problem getting a clean recording of the principal's voice. On the school website Mr. Parrish post videos of his weekly "Spring Creek Update." However, getting Jacardia talking in a quiet atmosphere would be a challenge. Add in me, holding my phone up to her mouth to ensure a recording that met my son's audio parameters and we're talking weird. This meant I was forced to resort to doing something I swore I would never do again - - write a *Closet Confidential* feature story.

Earlier, I mentioned that I was a freelance-writer which means I write everything from corporate newsletters (snoozer) to magazine articles. For three years I wrote a monthly feature for a local lifestyle magazine called *Closet Confidential*. Yes, it was as bad as it sounds. I interviewed women who had closets bigger than my first home. I would be "treated" to a guided tour by the shopaholic-of-the-month as she proselytized about earth shattering things like having a "denim bar" and glass cabinets to store her collection of Chanel handbags. All of these women must of shared the same decorator because every closet was decked out in crystal chandeliers and some sort of animal print carpet, usually leopard or cheetah. Every once in a while someone would step outside of the box and be daring, by going with, OMG, zebra!

It was while doing my thirty-seventh *Closet Confidential* interview featuring Charity Turner (think brunette version of Jacardia with substandard veneers. Why do some women spend a fortune on getting enormous boobs and then skimp on their dental work?) that I snapped and acted less than professional. I would argue, in my defense, that I was performing a much needed addiction intervention especially after Charity showed me the "denim boutique" area of her closet. It was floor to ceiling cubbies stuffed with 176 different pairs of jeans separated into categories. There were slim cut, boot cut, cropped, capris, toothpick, flared, boyfriend, low rise, trouser, dark wash, light wash, faded, sand blasted and vintage sections. I took one long look and pronounced Charity insane with a capitol I.

I was on a roll so I didn't stop there. I ventured on to explain that I was super certain any mental health advocate, primary care physician, or even a Walgreen's pharmacy tech, would diagnose her as a well-organized hoarder with psychotic shopping tendencies (probably manifested by king size daddy issues where the lack of paternal love she felt as a child is reflected in her retail expenditures). I also felt sure that her huge denim collection was how she compensated for what was most likely a less than satisfying sex life. Instead of thanking me for what I felt was an insightful and spot on diagnosis, she freaked and threw me out of her house! After that, she called the editor of the magazine and said I had "verbally abused her." I told the editor, Abby Rios, that, "Yes, I 'abused' Charity Turner if you define abuse as deeply caring about someone's mental health." As you can probably guess, I was fired from writing the *Closet Confidential* monthly feature.

Now, due to my need to get up close and personal with Jacardia, I'm going to attempt to get my *Closet Confidential* credentials reinstated. This means a phone call to Abby where I plan on telling her that I'm a changed woman and would love, love, love to do more hard hitting journalism from the front lines of lifestyle reporting - a spoiled woman's closet.

Abby picks up her phone on the first ring. She seems glad to hear from me and we talk about our kids for the first five minutes. I have a lot of respect for

Abby. She bought a failing magazine and in eight years has turned it into the local "must read." She's also gorgeous. Besides the inane closet feature, the magazine does a great job of covering the community. Before I even have a chance to ask for my favor, Abby says, "So, why are you really calling me?"

"Ouch, Abby, that hurts! I call you all the time and not just when I want something."

"Alright, I'll give you that, but it's the sound of your voice. It's too nice. Sweet even. That means you want something."

"What? I can't be sweet? I can be sweet. I'll have you know I'm sweet. I'm a very sweet person."

"No you're not, but that's part of your charm. So, what's up?"

This is when I decide to just go for it. I was going to hem and haw for a while longer, but she's on to me, so what's the point? I say, "I need a favor."

"Here we go. I knew you wanted something. What kind of favor?"

"A big one. I need you to let me write a *Closet Confidential* on Jacardia Monroe."

Abby starts laughing so hard I'm hoping she's not driving. It sounds like she's having problems catching her breath or choking on a Starbuck's Vanilla Almond Biscotti. "Abby, Abby," I say. "Are you okay?"

"Yeah, I'm fine and no you can't write another *Closet Confidential*. That Charity, what's her name, threatened to sue the magazine. I had to send her

70

flowers AND increase her *Closet Confidential* spread to six pages to calm her down. Six pages on a closet! Do you know how much ad revenue that cost me? There must something about you that ignites the fuse on all the crazies."

I took that as a compliment that Abby considers Charity crazy and not me. So, I forge ahead.

"What if I promise to be on my best behavior? Did you know I'm a graduate of the Central Texas Chapter of the White Glove Protocol Society for Southern Belles?"

"One, no, I did not. Two, you're not in Texas anymore. Three, what is the White Glove Protocol Society?"

"It's something all Alamo County Texas mother's force their thirteen-year-old daughters to do in hopes that by attending they'll magically become less moody, not confuse their shrimp fork with a salad fork and, fingers really crossed here, become Queen of the Mohair Palace Pageant material."

"Mohair Pageant? You're making that up. Is it a beauty contest or something?"

"Oh, it's a contest all right," I say in my best Southern Belle voice, "built around whose mother kisses enough butt so her daughter can be deemed possessing the correct amount of cash and family social standing to be crowned Queen of the Mohair."

I then switch back to my normal voice with a soupcon of begging, "Let's get back to me - present day. Think about it. Is it really fair to judge my whole writing career on one, very brief, lapse of judgment? To this day, I still feel like I was doing a public service by trying to get Charity to seek medical attention and because I respect you so much I'll write the article for free!"

I knew I had a good chance of getting my way when she got quiet. Abby didn't turn around a failing magazine by being a bad business woman. She was all about the free.

"Alright," she sighs. "You can do it, but you have to behave and I need it by next week."

"Yippee," I'm thinking! Then I go in for another favor. "Just one more thing - can someone besides me call Jacardia and set up a time for the interview? It would also be great if whoever calls could keep it on the down low that I'm going to be the reporter."

"You're killing me Wynn," Abby says sounding slightly ticked off. "Yeah, I can get my assistant to make the call. I don't know what you've got up your sleeve, but whatever it is it better not come back to haunt me. Got it?"

"Totally, now don't worry and just sit back in that comfy editor's chair of yours and wait for a scintillating, FREE piece on a freaking closet!"

Abby huffs and puffs a little while longer about "having a bad feeling" about the interview and then we get off the phone. I treat myself to a fresh Diet Coke and begin imagining what Jacardia's face will look like when I show up at her door.

Week Three of the School Year

Back In the Closet

It's Monday morning. I'm congratulating myself that less than a week after the PTA meeting I'm standing outside Jacardia's front door ready to begin investigating what's going on between her and the principal. Waiting with me for the door to open is the magazine's photographer Luke, who looks like he's just passed his drivers' license test. Alongside him is his surly, "I've slept in my clothes" protégé Teresa, whose tattoos even look grumpy. Abby's assistant had told me that when she called Jacardia to see if she would be available on Monday to be featured in the magazine, Jacardia freaked out and screamed, "Yes, yes, yes!" I wasn't surprised. For a certain caliber of late 30 to 50 something females, being interviewed in your closet is THE sign that you have made it. Think of it as the gateway drug to a *Real Housewives* gig.

Jacardia's housekeeper, still wearing the maid costume from the Halloween Super Savers store, finally answers the door and ushers us into the thirty-foot ceiling foyer where all the pictures on the wall are of Jacardia. Wait, I take that back. There is one picture of her two daughters, but no photos of her husband, or any family portrait in sight. I have a theory about this: I think Jacardia's husband is in organized crime. He seems lethal and he's all beefy, like he's been working out in a prison gym where it's all weights and no cardio. She says he's a hedge fund king, but you hardly ever see him. A year or two will go by and there's no visual of her husband. Could it be he's doing some hard time in a correctional facility?

We wait. It takes at least another five minutes for Jarcardia to regally descend down the stairs. When she finally makes her appearance she looks like a rainbow wearing a bad blonde wig. Jacardia is styling a super short orange dress with a tight, purple blazer that looks like it might have been bought in the girls' department at J.C Penny's. She's accessorized with so much jewelry she jingles jangles every time she takes a step down the stairs in her leopard-print sandals. (If I didn't know better I'd swear she has on spurs.) When she gets to the last step she announces, "The shoes are "Louboutin and the rest is all Stella."

This announcement baffles me for about two-seconds because my grandmother's name is Stella. Is my grandma making clothes? Then my *InStyle* magazine reading comes to the rescue, and I realize she means Stella McCartney, daughter to Paul and BFF to Gwyneth P. Jacardia is being trailed by her own hair and makeup team. I'm hiding, kind of, behind the photographer and at first she doesn't see me. When her left Louboutin hits the marble foyer I pop out and say, "Wow, you're looking good Janet! I can't wait to see your closet."

Talk about a mood killer. Jacardia's smile disappears and she makes a face like she was forced to consume a Cinnabon against her will. "Whaaat, are you doing here?"

"I'm the reporter and this is Luke the photographer, and Teresa his assistant."

Keeping it all business I add, "I think we should do the interview first. That will give Luke and Teresa time to set up the lights in your closet for the photo shoot."

"Wait a minute. Are you telling me I have to talk to you?"

"Um yeah, if you want to be the October *Closet Confidential* you have to talk to me, but if you've changed your mind, no worries. We can always get someone else. There's a huge list of women who want to be featured in the magazine, isn't that right, Luke?"

Luke, who has been enjoying watching the sparks fly, picks up on my cue and says, "For sure. There's a, what do you call it? A notebook, a big notebook, of women who want to be profiled."

I give him the smile I bestow on my kids when they use good manners out in public and say, "So, what's it going be? Do you want to do this or not?"

"Of course, I'll do it. I just wish they had sent someone who (she looks me up and down) knows something, anything really, about fashion."

I should be insulted, but I know I look fine by my standards. I have on my go-to-work uniform: Black pants, a patterned blouse and a very nice cardigan sweater from J Crew. Does it matter if it was 50% off? No, it does not. Also, I'm having a most excellent hair day. Thank you Suave shampoo and conditioner. I roll my eyes, ignore the remark and try to move things along by saying, "Why don't you show us your closet? I'll ask a couple of questions and then it will be all about you and your photo shoot."

The "all about you" got Jacardia's attention and I interpret her preening in the foyer mirror as a sign that we're good to go. Before she can complain about me some more I head for the stairs, but Jacardia body blocks me at the first step.

"Am I going in the wrong direction? Is your closet not upstairs?" I ask.

"Yes, it's upstairs, but first you and those two (she points to Luke and Teresa) have to put on shoe covers and hair caps."

"What!?"

As I'm acting as indignant as possible the housekeeper shows up with three paper shower cap looking things and three pairs of paper-shoe booties.

I sarcastically ask Jacardia, "Does your closet double as an operating room? Is there a plastic surgery clinic upstairs? Are you giving flu shots. If so, that's going to make a really great feature story."

"No!" She snaps back, like she finds my existence exhausting. "But the hair and shoe cover ups are still a must-do. I don't want bed bugs or lice in my house."

"Janet, that's just plain weird and wrong. Bed bugs and lice can come in on people's clothes. So, your shower cap and shoe bootie plan is flawed."

"No, it's not. I know by keeping people's shoes and heads covered it will cut down on body filth."

"Are you saying we're filthy? Plus you just had more than hundred women in your home last week for the PTA coffee. You didn't make anyone wear a shower cap then."

"True, but no one was going up to my closet. If you want to go up to my closet, my couture sanctuary, you have to put on the booties and the cap," Jarcardia says, while tapping her Louboutined toes.

"What about your beauty crew? They don't have on shower caps and booties."

"I know them and I know they're clean. I don't know those two and I know you well enough to insist you put this on."

Oh my God! I want to march right out her door. No, worse I want to take a dump in her black and white marble-tiled foyer and say, "How's that for body filth?" But, I calm myself. I have a mission to accomplish and if that means putting on paper booties over my shoes and a shower cap over my good-hair-day hair, then so be it. I walk over to Luke and Teresa and whisper, "Just suck it up and do as she asks. Your revenge will be taking pictures of her that make her look at least 10 years older and 20 pounds heavier."

Luke smirks and I see Teresa smile for the first time. I wink at both of them and say, "Okay, okay, we'll put on the protective gear. Give us a second and then lead on."

I pride myself on being a person who is rarely stunned but Jacardia's closet has my mouth gaping open and I feel a bit wobbly and nauseous like the time I ate two boxes of Thin Mint cookies while watching a *Mob Wives* reunion special. It might be the hot pink walls, or the ocelot inspired polka-dotty, striped carpet, (I will give her points for originality. She dared to go outside the traditional tiger family of carpets.) Or it may be the four blinged out mirrored crystal chandeliers, or the three floor-to-ceiling boudoir portraits of Jacardia dressed in lingerie apres her latest breast augmentation. While pushing the paper cap that keeps slipping down my forehead back up, I ask "Just how big is this closet?"

"Bigger than yours that's for sure," she chuckles and continues, "My closet, as you've probably guessed is all custom. Everything was made just for me. I told the architect to think big, really big. After all, I have a clothing collection to display. What you see is not a closet but a work of art. The exact square footage is a little over 1,500 square feet."

It's taking all the self-discipline I've ever possessed and everything I've ever learned from the Central Texas Chapter of the White Glove Protocol Society for Southern Belles to not say, "Are you shitting me? A 1,500 square foot closet? Have you never heard of Goodwill?"

Because now that I'm on my 38th Closet Confidential I can tell you with absolute certainty these women never throw out or donate anything that's ever been on their backs. They don't do the seasonal closet purge. You know, the three-pile method: keep, donate, and mend. They just keep, shop, and shop.

After I have composed myself by almost biting my tongue in half, I say to Jacardia. "Give me a second to set up my recorder thingy and then why don't you take me around your closet and describe how you've organized it. Then we'll finish up with what's your favorite thing."

I had taken the family iPad with me. My son had showed me how to hook up something called a "snowball microphone" to the back of it. The microphone was on a little tripod and it really did look like an extra-large snowball. I asked Clay why I just couldn't use my phone. He did the ticked off geek thing, and lectured me on the superior recording qualities of a professional USB mic. As soon as I plugged everything in and positioned the mic towards Jacardia I give her the thumbs up.

That's all it takes for her to chatter non-stop for twenty minutes. Jacardia's favorite word is big. Her favorite way to talk about her closet is using various riffs with the word "big" as in: "It's so big. I like it big. I want it bigger." My eyes start glazing over at about nine minutes in when I get a look at her workout clothes closet. Who knew yoga pants should always be stored on hangers and never folded? Folding, in case you're curious, causes "compression ridges in the lycra." And it's not just my eyes that are having problems. The smell of Jacardia's closet is searing a hole in my nasal cavities. I start wondering if you can file for workers' comp based on losing your sense of smell. She finally shuts up long enough for me to ask her, "Do you have like 1,000 Bath & Body Works' wallflowers plugged in, because it's *muy* fragrant in here?"

Jacardia laughs at me and says, "Bath & Body Works', hardly. When we were building this house I had a special air circulation feature put in the closet. What you smell is my signature scent, blended in Paris, of course, being misted at ninety-second intervals."

"Signature scent - my ass. Her closet smells like the hideous Twilight Woods from Bath & Body Works'. "How did you determine what your scent would be?" I ask her.

Of course I'm thinking she determined it by using a "buy one, get five free" coupon and stocking up on Twilight Woods at B&BW.

"I worked with a world-famous expert in the field of "parfum" who determined my aroma profile from 150 different scent emotions."

I roll my eyes at the olfactory wizardry of "scent emotions" because right now, I'm telling you, the only thing I smell is crazy. Jacardia goes on to further explain her "fragrance personality."

"Monsieur Perfumer said I smelled 'rich' (she touches her wedding ring), 'exotic' (she flips her hair), and 'sexy'" (she grabs her boobs). (Okay, not a grab really, but I'm telling you there is a brief moment when she aggressively fondles her right boob.) So together we both sniffed, whiffed and mixed until we got what the perfumer called (she pauses dramatically) 'the essence of Jarcardia.'"

Finally why some perfume is called "toilet water" is explained.

"Will this be in my article?" she asks. "I think it should. I don't know of anyone else in town that has their own scent."

"For sure, I'll put it in the story. It's one-of-a-kind fascinating. Now, why don't you show me your favorite thing," I say in a rush to move things along. I feel a headache coming on from "eau de Jacardia."

Jacardia doesn't let me down. She does what all the *Closet Confidential* women do when asked this question - lie.

In an attempt to sound normal and down-to-earth instead of having multiple psychological disorders the C.C. ladies make an effort to pick one heartfelt thing like a macaroni necklace their child made for them in preschool, or the first gift or clothing item they ever got from their husband. The problem with their made-up answer is when you ask to photograph them wearing the macaroni necklace or holding the L.L. Bean Fair Isle sweater their then boyfriend/not-yet-husband got for them in 1994 they can't seem to find it - ever.

Jacardia, flutters her mink eyelash extensions, puts her right hand on her heart and says, "My favorite thing is all the flower petals I saved from every bouquet of roses my husband has ever given me."

I try not to gag and end up coughing while asking Jacardia the necessary follow up questions. "Oh, how romantic. Do you mind if we take a picture of the rose petals? Do you keep them in a box or do you press them in books?"

I then settle in for the stall. This is where the C.C. ladies need a couple of minutes to figure out what story they're going to spin to explain why they won't be able to find whatever it is they just told us was their very most favorite thing in the whole wide world. Right when I'm about to start playing Scrabble on my phone, Jacardia says, "You can't take a picture of the petals. They're not here."

"Really, where are they?"

"They're being cleaned."

"You're cleaning dried up rose petals?"

"Um, yes, um because, um. . ."

Only due to my wish to not spend a minute longer than I have to trapped in Jacardia's closet wearing a paper cap, booties and breathing her essence, I throw her a bone and say, "Oh, I bet you're preserving them, like a historical preservation treatment, right?"

She smiles, "Yes, that's it exactly."

"No problem. Luke's got enough to work with here," I say while gesturing to the colossal closet. "And I've got all I need, so I'm going to show myself out and Luke and Teresa can start working on your photo shoot."

Jacardia's says, "Excellent. I'm all talked out and really won't the pictures tell the story? My closet is the stuff of legends. I have women calling me all the time begging for a tour. I even donate 'champagne tours' of my closet to charity auctions. It always goes for top dollar."

"Fascinating," I tell her while I unplug the mic, shove it in my purse along with the iPad and sprint out of the closet. Picking up speed I run down the stairs, head for the door and don't slow down till I get to the safety of my minivan. Once inside, I take off my cap and booties and save them to show to ABC, Nikki and Kelly so when they say, "No she didn't!" I can whip them out and say, "Oh yes, she did!" After I've restored my good-hair-day-hair, I take a couple of deep breaths of what I call normal air. Air that smells like fermented French fries, soccer socks, spilled Capri Suns, and dog dander with an overlay of Gain Febreze. I'll gladly take that scent any day over "eau de Jacardia."

Ready to Roomba

I could hardly wait to pick my kids up from school. I get Clay first since the junior high gets out earlier than the elementary school. As soon as he gets in the car I hand him the iPad and say, "I got at least twenty minutes of blah, blah, blah from Mrs. Monroe. Do you have time to do the whole vocal recognition thing this afternoon?"

"Maybe."

"What do you mean maybe? Do you have a lot of homework?"

"No, I mean maybe I'm too hungry to do it."

"Are you attempting to blackmail me for food?"

"Blackmail is such an unpleasant word. Let's just say I could use a Chipotle Burrito, with a side order of chips and salsa, sooner than later."

I look over at him, shake my head and say, "Okay, burrito it is and then you promise you can get everything set up for me. I'm on a deadline and I want to gift Mr. Parrish with the Roomba tomorrow."

"Sure Mom," he smiles, "as long as I get my burrito, you'll get your Roomba."

It took Mr. Smarty Pants all afternoon and into the evening to rig the Roomba. When Clay is finished he calls me into his room and shuts the door. I remind

83

him no one else is at home but the two of us. My husband is at a city council meeting and Grace is at a ballet class.

"You know you're a little paranoid for a 13-year-old?" I tell him.

"Sometimes paranoia is just having all the facts. William Burroughs."

"Huh?"

"The author William Burroughs said that. You've never read William Burroughs?"

"No, I mean, yes, I mean maybe, sometime, probably college." I make a mental note to Google William Burroughs and say, "So, Mr. Paranoid is everything ready?"

"Yes, but I have some concerns. Do any law enforcement agencies have your fingerprints on file?"

"Good Lord! Of course no law enforcement agencies have my fingerprints! You need to stop over thinking this. I'm just a mother who's giving a principal a gift."

"I've been thinking, sorry, over thinking, that you giving Mr. Parrish the Roomba is not a good idea. My suggestion is that you leave it in his office."

"Why is that better?"

"Because, everyone knows what a neat freak Mr. Parrish is and he won't be able to resist the Roomba. When he does find it in his office he won't be like,

"Hey why is there a Roomba in my office? Someone call the custodian." He'll be all, don't ask, don't tell because he won't want to share the Roomba. I'm telling you Mom just putting it in his office is the way to go and best of all, if things go bad you have no connection to the Roomba."

I think about this for a couple of seconds and say, "I agree. You're right."

He grins at me like I was a four-year-old who just spelled cat correctly.

"Now," I said, "all I have to do is get into his office with the Roomba without being seen."

That is no small task. The principal's office is protected by a Def Con 5 security force field. It's comprised of the school secretary, the office assistant and the school nurse. You have to navigate past all three of their prying minds to make it to the principal. I need a way to get those three plus the principal out of the front office to plant the Roomba. An idea came to me in an instant and I knew I would need ABC's help to pull it off. Kelly is too much of a good girl. She gets very nervous breaking any rules and Nikki is too inexperienced navigating the rough and tumble world of the suburban elementary school hierarchy to pull this off. Plus, I know ABC would gladly commit perjury for me. Bonus, we both look good in orange if prison jumpsuits were going to be in our immediate future.

I kiss the top of my son's head, leave his room and call ABC to see if she'll be available for a little morning espionage.

ABC is in as soon as I tell her the plan. She's designated the official Roomba courier. We agree to meet in the school parking lot at 7:30 the next morning.

85

Which works perfectly for me because I have Parent Patrol duty that begins at 7:40. I tell her to bring an extra backpack from home for Roomba disguise and transport.

The next morning is cloudy with a smattering of what I call sprinkle showers, more of a mist than a rain. Which means one thing - Parent Patrol duty will be hell. God forbid any kid gets a drop of water on them while exiting a car and walking fifteen yards into the school. Mothers will be doing everything they can to get their kids as close to the entrance as possible. If it means hopping curbs, cutting in line and putting their cars in park, blocking the flow of traffic so they can personally act as a moisture shield and escort their bundle of joy, rain drop free into the building, then so be it.

I'd be dreading doing my turn as school traffic cop if I wasn't so pumped up about the Roomba placement. In an effort to keep my daughter's nose out of my business I have asked my husband, Sam, to drop both kids off at school this morning. The last thing I need is super sleuth Grace asking a lot of questions like: Mom why did you give ABC a Roomba? Why did she put the Roomba in a backpack? Isn't that Clay's robot Roomba?

The reason I give Sam for having him do the school drop off duty is the fact that I have to go up to the school much earlier than usual due to Parent Patrol. "This way," I tell him, "the kids don't have to hurry through their breakfast."

As everyone is enjoying fruit and cereal I say goodbye. I'm thinking I've made a clean break for the garage until my husband gets up from the table and follows me.

"What's really going on?" he asks.

The good news is he's smiling and he's got a really great smile.

"What's going on is I'm headed to Spring Creek Elementary to risk life and limb doing Parent Patrol in the rain. Keep your fingers crossed some demented mother doesn't run me over."

"You're doing something else besides Parent Patrol. I've got a strong suspicion you're up to something."

"Oh, really?"

"Oh yes, you're showing all the signs - long phone conversations with ABC, a definite spring in your step, flushed cheeks, and you're deviating from your routine. All indicators, my beautiful wife, that you're in scheme mode."

He almost had me confessing my plan with the beautiful wife comment, but I stay strong and coo, "I will not confirm or deny anything you just said. All I will share is that you have nothing to worry about."

"So, that's how you're going to be," he says while leaning in closer to me. "Just remember I will not cash out our 401 K's to pay for your legal defense fund" and with that he kisses me.

I take the kiss as his way of telling me I have his blessing to do whatever I want. Before he can ask any additional questions, I hop in my minivan and gun it out of the garage.

ABC is waiting for me in the school parking lot. When I pull up, I motion for her to get in my car. We're both wearing similar outfits, track pants, hoodies and tennis shoes. She is also, like me, kid-free. After our phone conversation last night, she called her ex-husband and asked him to take the kids to IHOP for breakfast and then school. Living with divorced dad guilt, he eagerly said yes.

"Where's the spy vacuum?" she asks smiling, as she climbs into my passenger seat holding a Spider Man backpack.

"It's in the Whole Foods bag. Here, take it out and give it to Spidey."

ABC gives the Roomba the once over and says, "It just looks like a Roomba. I can't believe it's stuffed with video and recording stuff?"

I smile back on at her and say, "You dare to question the robotic ingenuity of a thirteen-year-old? For shame!"

ABC still inspecting the Roomba says, "Lookie here, your boy has quite the eye for detail. He's even put a school I.D. tag on it. How clever, now Mr. Parrish will think it's definitely from the district's custodial department."

We both laugh and ABC says, "This should be the most fun I've had before 8:15 in the morning in a long time."

"Are you ready then?"

"I'm ready. I feel almost James Bondish, I'm so ready."

"Then let's start with the phone call."

ABC takes a cheap looking, low tech, flip phone out of the Spider Man backpack and starts punching in numbers as she clears her throat. "Hello, is this Mickey's Towing? Hi, I've got a situation at Spring Creek Elementary that's threatening public safety at the school. We'll need two tow trucks ASAP to the staff parking lot. What's that? Why yes, I'm an authorized representative of the school requesting assistance. Thank you and hurry!" She hangs up, smiles at me and says in her best game show host voice, "Mickey's Towing, the official towing company of the school district, is on the way and in further news there's no way anyone can easily trace who made the call."

ABC is an aficionado of burn phones. During her acrimonious divorce, she attempted to alleviate her hurt and betrayal by utilizing all forms of cell phone harassment on her cheating spouse. It was during this time period she discovered the joys of the almost untraceable burn phone.

"That means you and the Roomba need to head for the office and I'll go get my Parent Patrol jacket on."

"Where do you want to meet up?" ABC asks. "The usual place?"

"Yes," I say as we both get out of the car, "Target, 8:25."

"Good Luck" ABC says, laughing, and then we each go off in different directions. ABC jogs to the office while holding the Spider Man backpack and I head to the teacher workroom to grab a neon yellow Parent Patrol jacket.

Parent Patrol

If you want to observe class wars, mom cliques, clueless drivers, and people who think their needs outweigh your child's safety then all you need to do is head to any suburban elementary school located near a country club, private tennis facility or Pilates studio between 7:45 and 8:15 in the morning. Once there you'll also get the chance to play *Hot Mom Car Bingo*. In this version of bingo the center square is, of course, the Escalade. The Escalady is as common to an elementary school morning drop off scenario as a $128 Vera Bradley backpack for a kindergartner. The other squares consist of the Lexus SUV, the Land Rover, the BMW SUV, the Denali, the Suburban, the big ass Infiniti SUV, loaded Sequoia, Porsche Cayenne and there's always one Mercedes-Benz G-Class. That bad boy costs well into the six figures and it's giving all the other mom cars the middle finger. These cars and their occupants will soon be pulling up to Spring Creek Elementary. As a Parent Patrol volunteer my goal is to assist children as they exit their parent's car and proceed inside the building. Trust me; all this is much harder than it sounds.

As I walk into the teachers' workroom to get my Parent Patrol windbreaker I'm thrilled to see my co-Parent Patroller of the day is Heather Farro. Heather is stocky with short brown hair that fits her no-nonsense personality. She thrives on putting up with zero bullshit and swears almost as much as ABC. We became fast friends three years ago while coaching kids' recreational soccer together. It was after the second game of that season we started a league-wide betting pool called "Who's Bitching at Us Now." All the coaches, before the start of the game, would bet on which parent they thought would go psycho. The best case scenario was the parent who would express the extreme displeasure that their child, "a profoundly gifted first grade athlete," did not receive more playing

90

time. Worst case was a dad getting up in our faces and screaming, "You suck, really suck at soccer! I don't know how you bitches can call yourself coaches." Never mind that Heather went to college on a NCAA Division 1 soccer scholarship and the Rec League has a strict rule that every child on the team is required to get exactly the same amount of playing time, when it came to their daughter's "soccer career" we were idiots. I usually won the betting pool every Saturday. Heather was always impressed by what she called, my "moron meter." I told her it was a skill I honed by attending family reunions.

Heather and her husband own a successful landscaping business, which is probably why this morning she has on khaki Carhartt overalls and, oh my, could those be steel-toed work boots?

"Heather, I gotta say, I love your boots."

"Thanks," she growls, "Last year, that Jacardia Monroe chick ran over my toes with her Range Rover."

"Oh my God! How awful! Were your toes okay?"

"They were bruised up pretty bad, but I could still move them. I'd have pitched a big fit, but they're clients of ours, so I sucked it up even though I can't stand her. To this day I have never received a freaking apology. She never even stopped her damn car. Scratch that - she never even slowed down."

"Seriously, she never even slowed down? Don't worry if anybody tries to run over you today I'll chase'em down for you."

"That, I have no doubt, you would do. Now, let's go outside and get this damn thing over with."

It's 7:45 a.m. School starts at 8:15. That means drop off traffic is at its worst between 7:50 and 8:10. We both march outside where the rain has picked up and get ready to greet the bad-mannered morning.

It takes less than five minutes before I let loose my first, "Holy Crap!" of the day. A Mom in a huge black Escalade with a massive custom bumper that looks like it's used to herd cattle or shopping carts on the weekends is accelerating toward me. She begins weaving through the other cars that are lined up to drop off their kids. Sweet mother of Slim Fast, she's not even looking in her windshield. All her focus is on her rearview mirror where she's putting on mascara and talking on her cell phone. How is she even steering?

"Slow down!" I scream, while waving my hands and jumping up and down looking like a mama kangaroo on meth.

If the SUV gets any closer I'll have its logo branded on my secondary roll of stomach flab. Oh no, oh no, she's jumping the curb and she s-t-o-p-s. I walk over to the car to give the mom a severe scolding.

Heather calls out to me, "Do you need help? Those Escaladys are a ballsy bunch."

"No, I've got it, thanks."

The pony-tailed Escalady rolls down her window just far enough to hand me her kid's backpack while she continues talking on her phone, never once making

92

eye contact with me. She then begins to roll her window up while my hand is still inside her car. WTF? I lean as much as I can into her window and say, "Excuse me, but you almost caused a serious accident and I don't appreciate you rolling your window up on my hand."

She gives me a "how dare you speak to me" look, puts down her cell phone and says, "I don't know what you're talking about."

"Well," I say, "I can see how you would be clueless because you're quite the morning multi-tasker - driving, talking on your cell phone and applying make-up, but you need to be more careful in the school zones."

I thought I was being nice considering she almost ran me over, but the Escalady disagrees. She puts down her phone and mascara wand and demands my name. "I'll have you know I'm going to text the school authorities about you harassing parents at the school drop off zone. I don't know who you think you are, but I won't be spoken to that way."

I really hate throw downs before I've had my first Diet Coke of the morning, but here goes. I calmly, yet with authority say, "My name is you better carefully back up and get out of here because you're holding up the line. Go ahead and text all you want because I intend to have the P.D. (That's police department. I like to use initials when I'm trying to sound tough. I think it makes me sound more official.) and the sheriff's department review the tape of your driving which, trust me, would qualify as endangering life and property. (Does the school have cameras at the school drop off area? No, but, I'm hoping she doesn't know that.) I slowly remove my upper torso from her car window and then she backs up off the curb and drives away, but not before flipping me the

93

bird. Really, the middle finger before 8:15 in the morning. Did she learn that at Escalady charm school?

Heather walks over and says, "I told ya." That she did, but I have no time to talk, more cars keep coming. I run over to check on a car that hasn't moved in a couple of minutes. For the drop off to be successful the cars have to keep on moving. It's called the "kiss and go zone." Parents are instructed to have their kids ready to hop out. If not, the school traffic backs up into a very busy street. A car that isn't moving is a bad thing.

As I get closer to the car that has parked itself in the drop off lane I hear a mom in distress. It happens, mothers lose it sometimes. The key is you've got to pick and choose where you're going to go non compos mentis and the school drop zone would not even make it to my top 100 list of places to have a breakdown. She's in full scream mode at her three kids. I knock on the window and ask if she can move her car. The kids have their hands on the car handle ready to jump out. I sense they are waiting for their mom to catch her breath and then they'll make their escape. I tell the mom, "Hi, the kids need to go or they'll be tardy and we need to keep the line moving."

She puts her head on her steering wheel and tells the kids goodbye. They haul out of that car like they're on fire. The poor mom begins weeping. I whisper, "Based on my vast experience, if you go up the street and drive inside the Exxon car wash you can sob your heart out. It's perfect because no one can hear you scream."

She nods and slowly pulls out of the line.

94

I take a moment to catch my breath and do a visual scan of the teacher and staff parking lot. No tow trucks yet. Where are they dammit? Just then I see the tow truck caravan turning into the school entrance. I take my phone out of the Parent Patrol jacket pocket, call ABC and whisper, "It's on."

I don't know why I whispered. It just seemed like the thing to do. I wanted to watch what I hoped was going to be a tow truck melodrama being played out, but I couldn't. The closer it gets to the bell the crazier it gets. It's all on ABC now to get the Roomba in position.

I make myself focus on being a traffic monitor. These parents are really pissing me off. The rain, as I predicted, has some moms in a precip frenzy. Murchy has blocked the flow of traffic by parking her Hummer with the personalized "HOLY1" license plates smack dab in the middle of the drop off zone. She gets out of her monster truck dressed in bike shorts and a bra top that says, "Prayercise." Murchy teaches a spin class at the gym that features 'inspirational" music in the form of Kirk Cameron singing the New Testament. She begins guiding her two daughters, in matching Hello Kitty umbrellas and rain boots, to the school's front door.

"Jen," I shout, "Your girls will be fine! You need to move your car!"

"Just give me five, will ya!" she yells trying to be heard over angry parents honking their horns because they're trapped by her Hummer. "I want to make sure my daughters stay dry!"

"You know girls are sweet and all, but I swear they're really not made out of sugar. They won't melt!"

Murchy runs by chanting, "And rain fell on the earth forty days and forty nights. Genesis 7:12"

Her comeback was quoting the Bible. Really? It's not like we're in the middle of an epic flood. It's barely raining and Murchy goes straight for Noah's Ark. I guess that's how she's going to excuse her hubris of parking her colossal car at such an angle in the drop off lane that no one can now move. "The Bible made me do it," is her defense.

I turn around as Heather says, "Watch this! Murchy left her car running."

She trots over to the Hummer, climbs in and lays on the horn. Heather then smiles, gives me two thumbs up, rolls down the windows and roars like Moses separating the Red sea, "The Lord has set me free!" She then drives the beast out of the drop off zone as parents stuck in their cars begin to applaud.

As Heather steers Murchy's Hummer over to the tow truck inhabited staff parking lot, I take a second to look over and see what's happening. "Yes!" I say, as I fist pump the air. It looks like the principal, the school secretary, the office assistant and the nurse are all arguing with the tow truck drivers. Awesome! ABC pulled it off. I'm telling you in a Zombie Apocalypse I want Heather and ABC on my team. I'm sure Heather, after running a landscaping company for 15 years, would be a freaking Samurai with a shovel.

After parking the Hummer by the tow trucks, Heather jogs back over. We high five and finish out the last couple of minutes of Parent Patrol. Just as we're about to call it quits and walk inside the school, Murchy runs up to us and screams, "My car! Where's my car?"

Heather looks around and says, "Your tank is right over there and it looks like it's being hooked up to the tow truck."

"Towed! Is my car being towed? Bitches."

She takes off to try to stop the tow truck driver, but not before giving us the bird.

Heather shouts back, "I bet they didn't teach you that in Sunday school!"

I tell Heather, "Wow, two middle fingers before 8:15. That could be a personal best."

"Not for me," she laughs and we attempt, again, to walk to the front of the school.

My hand is on the door when the Escalady runs up to me. You can tell she's itching for a fight. Heather says, "You want me to take care of her this time?"

"Stand down. I've got this one," I say in a voice I imagine using if I were leading a Special Ops troop in Iraq. I'm also psyched I got to say "stand down." I've always wanted to use that phrase.

"Is there something I can do for you?" I ask the Escalady.

She's wearing way-too-tight, hot pink velour Juicy Couture sweats with flip-flops that spell-out her first name in rhinestones and what I swear are false eyelashes. False eyelashes before 9 a.m. - my grandma would call that vulgar.

She looks me over, makes a face and utters my number two least favorite phrase in the English language. "Do you know who I am?"

I answer back, "I know you can't drive."

My five-word sentence launches her into temper tantrum. She recites her family tree in an effort, I guess, to illustrate her social superiority over me. Since I'm not that worried about launching my grade school daughter into society any time soon, I'm not overly interested in the Escalady's historic local lineage. What did she want me to do - curtsey? Like that's going to happen. I let her finish her tirade and then go in for the last word.

I take off my Parent Patrol jacket hand it to her (more of a shove into her face to be totally honest) and say, "Guess what? Tomorrow it's your turn. Have fun."

She stares at me, her collagen plump, overly glossed lips gaping open looking like a catfish I caught one summer at Girl Scout camp. Before the Escalady has a chance to say anything Heather and I turn our backs to her, walk into the school, and give each other another high five.

Since I'm no longer in custody of a Parent Patrol jacket, I tell Heather goodbye and sneak out the cafeteria side door to the staff parking lot. I can't wait to get to Target. Not only is a fountain Diet Coke with crushed ice waiting for me at the snack bar, but I'm dying to find out what went down with ABC.

On Target

Target is my happy place and Diet Coke is one of the great loves of my life. Is there much that compares to an icy, twenty ounce Diet Coke on an unbelievably hot and humid day? You grab that bad boy and run the chilly goodness of the bottle down your face, starting on your forehead and working the bottle lower to your lips. But, you don't taste it yet. You linger, savoring the delight to come and use the chilled Diet Coke to caress the back of your neck. Then, when you can't wait a minute longer, you open the bottle and taste the satisfying, thirst quenching, nectar of liquid chemical perfection, that is quite possibly (if you believe the emails my mother-in-law sends me) killing you with every swallow. As for Target, all I can say is if you've never experienced the sensual wonders of an intimate relationship with this handsome big box, then you haven't really lived. Just last month, I was walking down the aisle in the home furnishings section when I saw something I've coveted at Pottery Barn beautifully ripped off by Target at a fraction the price. I had to grip my shopping cart for stability as my body pulsated with waves of ecstasy. Thankfully, I had a large Diet Coke in my cart's cup-holder so I could extend my ride on the gratification surge by chasing the "moment" with a lusty swig. Talk about an afterglow.

I know most women enjoy meeting up at the sorority house known as Starbucks, but, I'm telling you, Target is the way to go. I walk in, inhale the smell of yummy, discount retail and head for the snack bar where I see ABC waiting for me. She jumps up and says, "I was amazing!"

"Awesome! Now don't say another word until I get my Diet Coke. I want to give you my full attention."

ABC patiently waits for me to order and pay for my drink. As soon as my butt hits the red Target snack bar chair she begins talking a mile a minute.

"Too much fun! I'm telling you it was too much fun! The whole thing has me considering giving up my career as a speech pathologist and becoming a spy. Do you think I'm too old to work for the CIA? Don't answer that. Oh, and I have to give kudos to you. Great plan. It went down just like you said it would. I thought Mrs. Shryock, the world's biggest pain in the ass school secretary, was going to pass out she got so mad. She was all like, 'Oh my God, don't touch my Camry! I just got it detailed at the Wash & Wax.'"

I'm smiling from ear-to-ear listening to ABC. It's been a long time since I've seen her so animated. Her divorce proceedings dragged on for almost two years and her self-esteem took a beating. It's like she was a beautiful heirloom rose bush that was brutally pruned with a hatchet. Slowly, I've seen signs that ABC might blossom again.

Laughing I say, "Slow down and start from the beginning. Remember, there's no such thing as too many details."

She takes two sips of her coffee purchased from the in house Target Starbucks, pats her lips with a napkin and says, "As you wish master."

I take another gulp of my Diet Coke and settle in for what I know is going to be a great story.

"Well, I did precisely what you told me. I remembered what my goals were: To keep everybody in the office and to find out where the principal is. Totally keeping to the plan I walked into the office and there was the principal's security trio; Mrs. Shryock, her side-kick Mrs. Li, and Nurse Cannon, who I think is getting married, again. Hasn't she been married like four times? Anyway, they're all standing behind that office counter eating what looked like zucchini bread. Yuck."

I interrupt her with, "No, not yuck. zucchini bread, if made correctly, is delicious, especially if it has a cream cheese, lemon sugar infused glaze"

"Good God, Wynn, if Betty Crocker or Duncan Hines ran a carbohydrate rehab center, I swear, you'd need to check in. Now, shut up and listen. This story is way better than damn zucchini bread. Oh crap, you made me forget what I was saying. Wait, wait, I remember. Okay, so you could tell all three of them were a little ticked that a parent was bugging them a whole thirty-nine minutes before school begins. Mrs. Shryock sighed in my face. I'm telling you, as far as sighs go it was a 'get the hell out of here' sigh. As you suggested, to engage them, I pretended to have an urgent issue that required the principal's brilliant guidance. Mrs. Li quickly shared that Mr. Parrish was on an important phone call and couldn't be disturbed. This was the information I needed - he was in his office. I know Mrs. Li thought that as soon as she told me the principal was *el ocupado* I would take off, but, following your instructions, I leaned on the counter and said, "That's too bad. Do you think one of you could help me? There's a situation with some of the Moms on the PTA board."

Of course, that was all it took to get their full attention. They even put down their precious zucchini bread. All three of them closed ranks around me and Mrs. Shryock told me to 'let my burden go.' That cracked me up. What did she think I was going to do confess to doing my children's homework for the past six years? Which, as you know, I would never do because (forget about the ethical considerations) I'm too damn lazy."

"What you call lazy I call good parenting, so give yourself a pat on the back and continue," I say.

"Well," ABC says nervously. "Now I've gotten to the part where I veered from our original plan. I guess you could say, I went a little off script."

"How off?" I ask.

"A lot off. I couldn't stop myself. Do you know how long it's been since I've had anybody's undivided attention, let alone three people's undivided attention? Sure, my divorce attorney listened to me, but only because I was paying her a lot for the privilege. Now that I had three women hanging on my every word I figured I ought to make whatever I was going to say sound really good, like juicy good."

"Regular juicy or super juicy?" I ask almost afraid to hear the answer.

"Oh, it was super juicy, the juiciest. I told them there is a rumor going around that the Spring Creek PTA is really a cover for a swingers club."

"What?! Do I need to remind you that our very good, very proper friend Kelly is on the PTA board."

"Calm yourself. I made it very clear not all the PTA board swung. Is that what you would call it, swung? Yeah, that's right swing, swang, swung. No, that doesn't sound right. Whatever. Now, put down your Diet Coke, I don't want you to spill it, because there's more. Are you ready for this? I said someone is claiming to have proof the PTA board isn't your everyday variety of swingers, but lesbian swingers. That's why they never let men on the board."

"Oh ABC, you did not!"

"Yeah, I did and it was great! They all stood there with their eyes bulging out of their heads and I could tell the gossip I dropped made their day, maybe their month. I have no doubt I'm their new favorite person for sharing that with them. Just wait till it hits the teachers' break room."

"You better hope this doesn't get back to Kelly. She'll kill you, no worse she'll have the IRS audit you. But, I must say, the more I think about," I take a second to rub my forehead, "I kind of like it. I totally can see Jarcardi and Murchy dating and going for couples' vajazzles and Katie Kirkpatrick would so go for Liz. It would be her version of an upwardly mobile hook up, getting it on with the PTA president."

I take another swig of Diet Coke and say, "Now let's get to what happened after I called and told you the two tow trucks had arrived."

"That was also excellent! As soon as I got your call, I told the office ladies goodbye and reminded them not to tell a soul a-n-y-t-h-i-n-g I had just shared with them, which, as you know, is a one hundred percent guarantee they'll start blabbing as soon as I turn my back. I do just that and walk out of the office, stop when I get to the big glass window in the front of the school, take my phone out and hold a fake conversation in case anybody is listening, then run back to the office and say, 'Oh my God, hurry and get the principal. There are two tow trucks in the staff parking lot and they're towing all of your cars. They said it was a public safety concern! I'd run out there if I were you and tell them to stop before they've got your cars all the way hooked up!'

Mrs. Shryock screams to the principal that all their cars are being towed. He hauls ass out of his office and they all high tail it for the staff parking lot. I pretend like I'm following them, but then turn around and make a break for Mr. Parrish's office. It's, of course, unlocked due to the distraction of the tow drama so I place the Roomba, very discreetly, under his desk so it might even take him a day or two to even notice."

ABC sits up very straight, smiles and says, "That's what I call mission accomplished. I hope you're impressed because I even impressed myself."

I smile back and say, "Great covert work! The CIA or any spy network would be very lucky to have you ABC. I'm sure there's a huge demand overseas for middle-aged, female spies."

"You forgot to add middle-aged, ass kicking, female spies. But, enough about the greatness that is me, when can we start eavesdropping?"

"Hopefully as soon as possible," I say. "I'm dying to know what's shaking with Jacardia and Mr. Parrish. Clay says the Roomba is rigged to alert his computer and begin recording when it hears both of their voices. I've got a feeling we'll get something to look at today. With Jacardia as the principal/parent liaison, I can't imagine her not needing a little private conference time with her brand new best friend."

Neighborly Love

ABC and I both left Target with smiles on our faces. I'm now home working. I need to write Jacardia's *Closet Confidential* today and I have a corporate employee newsletter that's due. It's all about a company's "team building" day which includes relay races with an egg. Here's a little advice for all the businesses out there: instead of forcing your employees to participate in team building exercises, why don't you give them a paid half day off and a couple of movie passes. That would do more for company morale than running with an egg on a plastic spoon from the break room to the receptionist's desk. I'm just about ready to write about the "good times" at A&S Manufacturing when my doorbell rings. Crap. When you doorbell ding-dongs at 10:00 in the morning, on a school day, you know it's never good. It means someone is trying to sell you carpet cleaning, maid-service, lawn-care, Jesus, or worse, your neighbor wants something. I trudge downstairs to answer the door and it's Kevin Kendall, "Mr. Super Family." What a bummer. Until now my day had been going so well.

"Hello, Kevin," I say in a less than enthusiastic voice. "What's up?"

Kevin Kendell is a petite, hairless man who resembles a turkey baster and is always dressed in black bike shorts showcasing a groin adjacent scorpion logo. He also favors Spandex tank tops that showcase his erect man nipples in a constant state of thrust. He sells insurance, I guess from home, because I've never seen him in long pants or a shirt with buttons. I'm beginning to wonder if he's lacking opposable thumbs and doesn't have the necessary digits required to master a button or zipper.

Kevin adjusts his tank top and says, "As you may know, Kandance and I have our 18th year anniversary coming up and I wanted to see if you'd like to play a part in our annual anniversary scavenger hunt? This year the theme is pirates."

Ahoy Matey, there is no way I was going to be suckered into taking part in their anniversary extravaganza. The whole thing is a howl for help and a plea for Class A pharmaceuticals. Every anniversary, Kevin sends his wife on a scavenger hunt around the neighborhood to find clues where to locate her present. This means that almost every neighbor is caught up in the drama of the gift hunt. It starts about a week before the anniversary with Kevin coming over to see if he can leave a hint at your house on such and such date and time for the scavenger hunt. When we first moved here I said yes, not knowing I was going to be enabling a couple in a sick marital ritual.

Kevin makes Kandance wear a costume that in some way is a tip off about her gift. She frolics (most often breathlessly) from door-to-door collecting clues in the form of little gifts, and then ta-da, she finally locates her mega present. By this time, a large portion of the neighborhood is following Kandance to see what her grand and glorious husband has surprised her with. Last year it was a Walmart (seriously) cruise for their anniversary. (Technically, it was a cruise bought through the Sam's Club, but everyone knows Walmart owns Sam's.) Almost every female neighbor, after this shameless bid for attention, always sighs and comments on what a romantic husband Kevin is. I keep my mouth shut and try to figure out what kind of unique hell is going on inside their two-story Tudor home with a finished basement to make a couple in their 40's take to creating an annual spectacle of themselves. Last year, Kandance was wearing a grass skirt and a way-too-small-for-her-boobs coconut bra when she went clue hopping for her cruise. Is it just me or does forcing your wife to wear a bra made

106

of fruit and a grass skirt constitute some form of spousal abuse? I'm thinking at the very least it's pain and suffering.

I tell Kevin, "Yeah, about your scavenger thing, I'm sorry, I think we're going out of town."

"But, I haven't even told when I'm planning the hunt!"

"Oops, that's right you haven't, but my whole September is super busy and you might want to check in with your wife. She probably doesn't want to come to my house for anything, much less her anniversary present clues."

"I know all about that. Kandance and I have zero secrets. We share everything. We're soul mates, bonded for life."

"Great, that means you're just like termites and black vultures."

"What does that mean?" he says, pissed.

"Termites and black vultures, they bond for life. Congrats, you're part of a nifty club."

"You've confused me," he said, giving me a look that told me he is often easily confused. "But just so you know, about last week, we forgive you."

"What?" I say. Now I'm confused.

"Kandance and I, being the, I don't want to say - 'bigger people,'" Kevin blurts out while giving me the once over.

Go ahead, Five Foot Four Inches Kevin, look all you want because beneath these track pants and hoodie is a woman who can bench press two 50 pound bags of Iams Proactive Health dog kibble and drop-kick your ass.

"But" he continued, "Being the more, I don't know, honorable family, we forgive you for what you did last week."

"Well, just so you know, here's a little FYI for you. I think we probably have different definitions of the word honorable and I don't need nor will I ever be seeking your forgiveness, but thanks anyway. If that's all, Kev, I need to get back to work."

"Yeah, that's all. Let me know if you change your mind about the scavenger hunt," he says while walking down my front porch steps. As he gets to the last one he stops, turns around and says, "You know you're about the only person in the neighborhood who doesn't play along?"

As I close my door, I say, "Like I said, Kevin, I'm busy, very busy. Bye, bye now."

Oh my God, Kevin and Kandance "forgive me"? What a crock. I did nothing wrong and everything right. I called his little Super Family out and it hurt their super cry baby feelings.

Here's the deal. Last week I offered up The Super Family a little quid pro quo by messing with their allegedly perfect little world. Kevin and Kandance truly believe with all their hearts and tiny, misguided brains, that their three (astoundingly annoying and average) children (ages 13, 15 & 16) are superior to all intergalactic life forms. Two of the ways they show this to the world is with yard signs and banners. Yes, when boasting on Facebook is not enough, by all means litter the neighborhood with signage. Different public and private schools fundraise with yards signs. The more crap your kid is involved in the more yard signs that clutter your lawn. For as little as $200 you can buy a yard sign that says your kid is on the volleyball team. For an additional fee you can purchase sign accessories with things like guitar club, performing arts, or even school comedy troupe. My neighbors have about two dozen of these signs in their yard. To add to their glory they also attach banners to their corner lot fence to share with the world just how incredible their children are. This week, I'm guessing in honor of the new school year starting, there's a banner that reads, *"Kelsey, Kaleb and Kacey, the reason teachers like to go to work in the morning. The best of the past, perfect in the present, and the hope of the future!!!"*

Now while this sign is an excellent example of their Stage Three Delusional Disorder, one of my favorites was two Saturdays' ago, when they had a banner that read: *"My Mom Just Ran Her 11th Marathon! What Has Your Mom Done Today?"* Too bad, good manners (well really my husband) prevented me posting a banner on my fence that said, *"This Mom Is About to Kick Your Mom's Ass."*

Never fear, I did get my ass kicking in. Last week, I managed to make their yard signs insignificant. I went on a faux yard sign rampage. You've got that right, I made up fake yard signs - 26 of them to be exact. It was so simple I'm ashamed of myself for not thinking of it earlier. All it took was my son to use his computer skills to duplicate the middle and elementary school logos, add a bunch of made up B.S., get them printed on card stock at Kinko's and then staple gun each "sign" to a stake purchased from Lowe's. Sure, it cost some money and I had to push back getting my hair highlighted for two weeks to fund this endeavor, (Why is color printing so expensive?) but it was worth it. The most enjoyable part was thinking up the bogus stuff to put on the yard signs. These are my favorites (I would be remiss not to give a shout out to my kids for helping think of all the captions): Most Tardies, Clean Locker Club, National Society of Halo Gamers, Class of 2018 Attendee, Mouth Breather Since 1999.

I also threw in some other signs. Ones that were more related to the parents who also had signage about their accomplishments, especially running marathons. Every time they completed a marathon a new sign proclaiming 26.2 went in their yard with the location of where they ran the marathon. Well, game on neighbors because I had my own 26.2 experiences. For sure, mine didn't mean I had run 26.2 miles, but I've lived a long life of 26.2. For example, 26.2 could mean the number of pounds I need to lose, or the 26.2 sleeves of Girl Scout Thin Mint cookies I could eat in a 26.2 hour period.

I waited and stuck the signs in my yard when my husband would be going out-of-town for three days. Like I needed his throat clearing disapproval act. On the outside he's all, "God, really? This is all so immature. Why do you care?" But, I know on the inside he's all, "You go crazy, wife of mine. You go!"

I put my signs in the yard late at night, so when the Super Family went running at 5:30 the next morning they would be greeted by my yard "art." I even set my alarm and perched in the upstairs window so I could watch them explore my lawn. Here's how it played out: I could see them jogging. They run by. Their heads do a whiplash move. They come to a screeching halt, walk into my yard and begin checking out all my signs. I can see their agitation and by that I mean they are visibly pissed off. Waves of thrilling happiness surge through my body as I witness this and experience a rather intense revenge orgasm.

Fast forward four hours and my doorbell rings. It's Kandance. Her brown hair is trapped in a Nike baseball cap. She's got on lime-green Dri-Fit running boy shorts, that look more like tight granny-panties than athletic wear, and a black Livestrong sports bra. She's very tanned and speckled. In fact, she looks like a bowl of Cocoa Rice Krispies. Sure, she's got killer abs, but advantage me, my love of baked goods and SPF 70, because my face, plumped with nature's Restylane (fat) looks ten years younger. I know she's come to comment on my signage. Kandance is especially riled up, of course, about the 26.2 signs. Now, when I say riled up, I mean she is behaving with a veneer of politeness. This is the suburbs, after all, and she's an active member in good standing of the Junior League and co-chair of the "Love Your Neighbor" initiative at her church, but I can tell it's k-i-l-l-i-n-g her. Her body language is saying, "I want to strangle you with my Adidas mesh-crotch running thong."

She comes into my house and says, "What's up with all your new signs?"

I act confused and bewildered and respond in a tone that says I'm as sweet as Texas tea at the Lions Club BBQ. Which means I give it right back to her with, "You have a problem with my signs? You have signs in your yard."

Kandance fires back, 'Well, my signs are what I would call legitimate. Yours seem to be all made up."

"Really?" I say, acting concerned, "Show me a sign out there that's not true."

"Oh, that's easy. When did you ever run a marathon?"

I was more than ready for this line of questioning. I sucked in my gut as best I can, which means one roll of flab receded, but the secondary roll remained at full sag, stood up straight and said. "Oh, I've run a marathon. A marathon of faith. While your 26.2 worships the miles you've run, my 26.2 worships the good book. Isaiah 26.2 *"Open the gates, that the righteous nation that keeps faith may enter in."*

Bam! You don't go to Baylor University for four years and have to suffer through Old and New Testament religion classes (which were incredibly difficult by the way) and something called Forum every Wednesday and not come out with some mad Bible verse skills. Don't try to out church me people. You will fail!

This, as I predicted, shut her down. She stammered and yet attempted to compliment herself all at the same time with, "Oh, I didn't even think of that. You know, as an acclaimed elite runner I see 26.2 and think marathon."

"Well, (insert me sighing and doing my best impersonation of my mother) not everything is all about you, is it? Now, I hate to rush you off, but I was just on my way to Bible study (and of course, for me, Bible study just happens to be Target, but is that any of her business? No.) and need to go tidy up a bit before I leave."

This morning my faux signs are still standing proud and tall in my yard. My husband even thinks they're funny, but I did promise him I would take then down when I decorate for Halloween in a couple of weeks. Since I'm downstairs, I decide to make myself a snack and then I've got to get back to work. Once the kids get home from school my day gets hectic. Grace has soccer practice, and the junior high is having their parents' back-to-school night. Plus, I have to attend family therapy at 7:30 with ABC. It's complicated.

112

Uggs vs Fuggs

Carpool is completed and I'm back at home with Clay and Grace. I ask my son to check and see if there have been any Roomba transmissions to his computer. Clay reports back (over his sister's whining that she can't find her soccer cleats) that so far nothing has been recorded from the principal's office. I'm disappointed, but not surprised. Maybe Jacardia was getting her weekly, pour-a-gallon-of-Clorax treatment on her marshmallow-white hair. I help Grace locate her cleats, grab her water bottle and load up for soccer practice. When we get to the field, Kelly sees me and runs over. She looks angry. I tell Grace to start doing some kick drills with Kelly's daughters to get the three of them out of hearing range. I turn to Kelly and say, "What's wrong? Period late?"

"What? No, thank God. Did you hear about this thing called the Majesty Club?"

"Majesty Club? No. What is it? A new diet fad, where someone invites me to their home, serves me a half-cup of room-temperature Franzia Chardonnay poured from a carafe to conceal their cheapness and a couple of slices of cheese and then tries to sell me a juice diet that will, "I promise," take fifteen pounds off in two weeks?"

"No. Worse."

"Really, worse than pretending you're having a party and then shaking down all your acquaintances and neighbors for cash?"

"Yes."

"I find that hard to believe, but do go on."

"Well, Sophia and Chloe came home today and were all upset over something called the Majesty Club. Apparently it's a new mother daughter organization at school where you have to be invited to join. All the little girls that are members of the club came to school today in T-shirts with a tiara on them outlined in rhinestones and matching hot-pink Uggs with bows on the back."

"If one of those little girls is Jacardia's daughter Aleexiah, then count your blessings that you and your daughters weren't asked to become a members of that club."

"Yes, I know that, but that's not what has me upset. The girls that are members were being cruel to the other kids. At lunch they were doing an Ugg versus Fugg contest."

"What the hell is that?"

"They were walking around the lunchroom pointing out girls who didn't have on Uggs, but were instead wearing boots that looked like Uggs. You know like Bear Paws or the Target suede kid's boot. To hear Chloe tell it, it was like a game of Duck, Duck, Goose, but instead it was Ugg, Fugg, Fugg."

"Those girls need to Fugg off. Where were the teachers when this was going on?"

"I don't know. I wasn't there. I'm hearing this all second hand from my girls. Although I did see the tacky T-shirts and Uggs when I picked up the girls from school."

"Kelly, I can't believe I'm the one saying this, but let it go. Who cares? The club sounds like an Al Qaeda training camp for mean girls. It's best to just keep your distance."

"I don't think so. This club needs to be looked into!"

Whoa, Kelly, I haven't seen you this fired up since the Tax Code was changed. What's really going on?"

"I'm telling you I don't like any of this one bit, least of all that this club is masquerading as a Mother-Daughter volunteer organization. When did excluding others, being mean, and acting like you're better than everyone else equal public service?"

"When the Junior League was founded in 1901," I answer back.

Kelly laughs and says, "You're never, ever going to let it go that you were kicked out of the Junior League are you?"

"Correction. First, I was passive-aggressively forced against my will *by my mother* to join the Junior League. Second, I VOLUNTARILY surrendered my placement name tag; Junior League apron; cookbook; exclusive, not-to-be-shared-with-the-general-and-lesser-public JL phone directory; and any claims and/or connections to the organization up to and including attendance at Junior League events, holiday fundraisers and charity galas. It really was more like I was banned for life, which is not like being kicked out - AT ALL."

"Sorry, my bad. You're right," Kelly says, still laughing. "You were totally not kicked out. What could I have been thinking?"

115

"Whatever, let's not talk about it. It's been five years, and it still ticks me off. So, when did you find out the Majesty Club is a volunteer group?" I ask. "I thought you said you just heard about it from your girls this afternoon."

"I did, and then I made some phone calls," Kelly answers, still fired up.

"Wow, you've found out this much information in under an hour. No wonder you're so good at your job."

"Thank you, and guess who the president of the Majesty Club is?"

"That's easy, the Majesty gave it away. It has to be Liz Derby."

"Yep."

"Which, Kelly, is one more reason you should be thankful you're not involved in anyway whatsoever with this club."

"Maybe, but I still think we need to do more investigating. You should put Grace on it."

"I don't know, Sam really doesn't like it when I involve the kids in things like this."

Kelly gives me a "You've got to be kidding me" look and says, "This isn't any big deal. It's information gathering and your daughter's good at it. It would be a sin not to develop her God-given talent."

"Well, when you put it like that what can I say but okay."

I look for my daughter on the field where she's doing cartwheels instead of kicking drills and yell, "Grace come here for a second!"

"What Mom?" she asks as she jogs over to us.

"Hey, little one, Kelly and I need a favor," I say as I hand her a pink water bottle. "Can you go all Nancy Drew for us and find out, without causing a fuss or drawing attention to yourself, thank you very much, everything you can about the Majesty Club?"

"That's easy, Mom! I already know a lot, but yeah, I can do it. Oh, I have an idea," she says while jumping up and down, "I can have a play date with Windsor and snoop around."

"That sounds great, honey, but please don't snoop, it's not polite. Just ask questions and listen."

I then notice her coach motioning for Grace to come and take her turn being the goalie. "Look, your coach wants you back on the field. Give me your water bottle and go play."

"Okay, awesome possum. I'll start the 'not snooping' tomorrow," she sasses and runs off.

Kelly smiles and says, "Grace may look like your husband, but she's got a lot of her mama in her."

Also smiling, I reply back, "I know. The day I caught her in bed eating bacon under the covers, I knew my DNA was starting to assert itself. Great idea, by the way, she had about getting a play date with Windsor."

117

"I told you your girl is smart and brave. She'll be going into the belly of the beast for that play date - Liz Derby's house. Yuck."

Kelly is right. Yuck, big time. Windsor is Liz Derby's youngest daughter. (Her full name is Windsor Tudor Derby. Liz says Windsor was named after their distant kin Queen Elizabeth. Liz's oldest daughter is 11-year-old Regina Viceroy. Liz says that's how the Queen signs her name.) The Derby home is 4,500 square feet of no fun. It's one of those 'don't touch' homes where, I swear, cross-my-heart-and-hope-to-die swear, there are velvet ropes, just like the kind in movie theaters, closing off rooms from any human interaction. The first time I went to Liz's home for a school meeting I was mystified by the whole rope thing and blurted out, "What's with the ropes?"

Liz was delighted to share that the ropes denoted "special occasion" rooms and only came down for "memorable family events."

My stunned reply was, "Really, those ropes work for you? Because in my house it would be a matter of my kids honor to not only go under those ropes on a daily basis, but to jump over them, take them down and catapult them at each other, and last, but not least, attempt sibling strangulation by velvet rope."

Liz smiled very smugly and said, "Different houses, different rules."

I was thinking, "That's for damn sure." Liz's velvet-rope theme also extends to her daughters' bedrooms. Friends are encouraged to play only in their basement. Which wouldn't be a bad thing because it's an American Girl paradise with tons of dolls and accessories. Except Liz is mega OCD about kids messing up anything. You go in the basement to look not to play. My daughter calls it the house where toys go to die.

118

In the middle of my deep thoughts how my daughter is really taking one for the team by going over to Windsor's house, I'm distracted by the arrival of my husband, Sam. He's looking world-weary handsome in his suit with his tie loosened. He's here to take over the night shift.

"Hi, honey, how was your day?" I ask.

"Pretty good," he says while laughing at Grace playing goalie and doing hand stands when the team is on the other end of the field. "So, go over with me again what the plan is for tonight?"

"After soccer you and Grace go get Clay and take him to his viola lesson. You'll need to pay his teacher $20. I've made crockpot lasagna so all you have to do is break out the garlic toast and you've got dinner. I'm going home to change, and then I'm off to the junior high's back-to-school night and after that it's therapy with ABC. I'm thinking I won't be home till after nine."

"Okay," he says as he kisses me on the cheek. "Have fun and good luck with therapy."

"Oh, I have no doubt therapy will be a blast."

Sam shakes his head, and Kelly and I laugh. I tell both of them goodbye and walk briskly to my minivan. I've got an interesting night ahead of me.

Therapy

Fortunately I'm a woman who can get showered, shampooed, blow dried and dressed in under forty minutes even if you add in extras like moisturizing my eczema patches with a lavender-scented prescription cream, spritzing myself with Gain Febreze and throwing back a "just in case" Gas X. (Due to a very vocal lower intestinal track that loudly protests any sudden movements or enthusiastic stretches. So, for me, that's a big no to Pilates and a hell no to yoga.) This all means I'm out the door for the junior high in record time which allows me to grab a Diet Coke at the Micky D's drive-thru. I figure I'll need the caffeine to stay alert during Back-to-School Night.

When Clay started junior high and begin the ritual of having a different teacher for each class the back-to-school night experience changed exponentially. No longer did I sit in one classroom and listen to one teacher expound on the exciting things that will be happening that school year. Oh no, now I get to spend almost two hours, in ten minute chunks, making a pilgrimage to each of his seven teachers classrooms. This explains why right at this moment I'm trying not to get stepped on by eager parents rushing through the crowded hallways trying to figure out where their child's first hour class is located.

Walking the hallways presents a disturbing visual feast, like a ten car pile-up on the interstate or me in shorts. You want to look away, but you just can't. The worst are the moms. If I had a bullhorn I'd use it right now and shout, "Attention All Mothers: Walking into a school does not magically turn back the hands of time. You are still middle-aged. Please dress like it."

It maybe just me, but I think if a school has a dress code the least the parents can do is abide by it and what's with all these moms in their workout clothes? I'm listening to two women wearing sports bras, (tsk, tsk, on that) brag how they worked back-to-school night into their running schedule. One said she just got done "road slamming thirteen miles." Okay, that's too impressive for me not to comment.

"Wow." I say. "You ran thirteen miles? How long did it take you?"

"Not that long, I'm in training for the New York Marathon in an effort to BQ."

Now she's talking a Texas girl's language barbecue so I say, "They have that good ol BBQ in New York City? That surprises me, but in a good way."

The marathon mom sneers at me and says, "God, how would I know. I don't ingest animal flesh. Besides I said B.Q. as in Boston Qualify. You know THE Boston Marathon."

I don't know why my little mistake made her so angry. It's not like I'm the one that smells like B.O. and is up at my kid's school in a freaking bra. Always one to take the high road, I say, "Oh, sorry" and then ask her just to be gross, "Hey, do I have any gristle in my teeth?"

Worse than the fashion is the parental behavior. Moms are walking down the halls giggling, talking on their phones, texting and screaming, "Hi!" and hugging when they see someone they know, like their neighbor, who they just talked to 15 minutes ago in the parking lot. It's resembles a gaggle of hyper-anxious geese or a collective group seizure. The dads are not as bad, but really gentlemen the fist bumps in the hall, the not so clever quips, it's all very unsettling. I've come prepared with my survival mantra. It helps me when I flashback to my tween and teen years. I take a few deep breaths and repeat, I am not in junior high school. I am a successful professional and parent. No one is going to yank on my bra strap or tell me I can't sit at their lunch table.

As I'm mid mantra ABC, who I haven't seen all night, comes over and whispers, "Prepare yourself here comes Katie with her little red wagon."

I burst out laughing. Katie, the Merry Sunshine of Sucking Up, is doing her signature back-to-school move of dragging a Radio Flyer red wagon filled to the brim with her "world famous chocolate chip pumpkin bread."

"How confused is she?" I ask ABC, "Who brings pumpkin bread in a toddler's wagon to junior high teachers? If she really wants to impress them she should be pulling a cart that's loaded with cases of wine. That's what I'd need to teach the hormonally surging."

ABC is having a giggle fit watching Katie. "I can't take my eyes off her," she says. "Do you see her stopping to ask people if they 'want to see what's in her red wagon'? It sounds like a bad porno."

We both shut up to listen to Katie as she explains to a couple of dads about the contents of her wagon. "The best thing I have in here is my pumpkin bread. I'm not fibbing when I tell you it is world famous. I've also got banana bread and these cute pencils. See," she says in a voice that sounds like a Disney Princess taking hits of helium, "I've even attached pencils engraved with 'The Kirkpatrick Family Loves Teachers'."

One dad, God bless him, tells her, "I can't believe you still do this. I know I've seen you pulling your wagon at the elementary school, but junior high, that's a whole different game."

Katie, of course, takes it as a compliment and asks all of us standing around, "You mean none of you bring goodies to the teachers? That's just unbelievable to me. They need our loooove."

Like we're bums or something for not plying our kid's teachers with food that I'm almost positive they don't want. I've hit my Katie quota so I reply, "No, we don't bring goodies because our kids have learned to stand on their own feet and don't need little pumpkin bread shoes to prop them up."

This leaves Katie looking stunned, which is not much different from her looking terminally happy. Thankfully, the bell rings and we all quickly walk into what is hopefully the right first hour class.

I'm out of the junior high in under ninety minutes. I decided to ditch the P.E. class. What can I say? Old habits die hard. As I'm driving to ABC's family therapist I'm practicing being pleasant to her ex-husband Jim. "Why, hello Jim. Good to see you. How is everything? Nice fall weather we've been having isn't it?" I say out loud, to myself. No, I'm not losing it, but I hate her ex so much I need to rehearse civility because what I really want to do every time I see him is kick him, repeatedly, in the balls.

If you're thinking it's because he's gay you couldn't be more wrong. I have no problem with anyone's sexual preference. I'm not pro or anti-gay. I'm anti-dumb ass and her husband is one gigantic dumb ass. I could care less about the whole same-sex thing. I mean why would I base my judgement of someone because of their sex life with another consenting adult? We spend more time brushing our teeth then we do having sex. Would I judge someone based on their oral hygiene? Well, that maybe a bad example because yes I would. What I do judge a married human being on is if they don't serially betray their spouse. I get it that Jim finally admitted to himself that he was gay. That's when he should have been brutally honest with ABC about what was going on and proceeded directly to Divorceville, but that's not what happened. For years, to hear Jim tell it, he wasn't quite sure if he was gay or bisexual so he went on an "exploratory quest." Translation he cheated on ABC with a variety of men and women for more than half of their married life. The health implications alone are terrifying. It was ABC who sued for divorce. That made Jim and his wallet very unhappy. He has and will be paying ABC a substantial share of his dermatology practice profits for a very long time.

The divorce caused ABC to have some, let's say, anger control issues. Jim says she tried to bludgeon him with a Pampered Chef marble rolling pin. Please, if ABC wanted Jim dead, trust me, she would have murdered him years ago and I would have helped her. The result of Jim's court filing about the attack of the killer rolling pin lead to these mandated family therapy sessions to help both of them "deal calmly with co-parenting issues." If that's not bad enough, last month Jim started bringing his boyfriend, Jasper, because Jim says, "Jasper is part of his family" to therapy. That's when I became ABC's plus one.

I pull up to the therapist office almost as the same time as ABC. I get out of the car and yell over to her, "You must have skipped out of back-to-school night early too. What class did you ditch?"

"Choir. I didn't want to run the risk of the teacher begging me to get Zack to drop her class."

"Why would she want him to do that?"

"Wynn, I can't believe you're asking me that question. You've heard Zack, my tone deaf son, sing".

"Oh yeah, he does suck at singing, but maybe choir will help."

"Not likely and look who's here - Old Dumb Ass with Younger Dumb Ass."

ABC's ex-husband, Jim, and his boyfriend Jasper walk over to us and we all make polite chit chat, just like I rehearsed in the car, as we make our way inside the therapists office. Jim looks like Malibu Ken. He's even got the whole plastic face down due to using too much of his dermatologist "juice" on his own forehead. If he puts anymore Restylane in his cheeks it will resemble a skateboard park, lots of concrete curves.

His boyfriend/family member Jasper is the male version of a trophy wife. Young, blonde and spray tanned. He works at Jim's dermatology office in the Medical Day Spa as the dude who does facials. He also talks in abbreviations, as in adorbs for adorable, totes for totally, sers for seriously etc. Is it wrong I want to slap him till his spray tan wears off?

We all get settled in on the sofas in Nancy Hernandez, Ph.D in Marriage, Family and Couple Counseling's office. My job for the next 50 minutes is to sit back and glare at Jim. Dr. Hernandez looks to be in her late forties and reminds me of an excellent kindergarten teacher. She talks slowly, smiles a lot and wants

125

everyone to feel good about themselves. Tonight Dr. Hernandez wants ABC and Jim to work on having consistent rules for their three boys, so she says, "No one is the bad guy."

This is one of those things that sounds good, but never works. In every family someone has to be the bad guy or as I like to say the enforcer. In my house, on a day-to-day basis, I'm the bad guy because I spend more time in the parenting trenches. This means I'm the one screaming, "Pick up your room!" every hour. I want to share this keen insight with Dr. Hernandez, but since I'm not the one paying for the session I keep quiet. Jim, who has always been deeply in love with the sound of his voice, starts going off on how ABC needs to discipline their three boys more effectively. This is where I earn my keep. I begin glaring at Jim, then I add in a smirking glare when he says something stupid. I switch back to the, never goes out of style, "You're a bigger dumb ass then I thought" glare and finish up with "My God, I can't believe anyone lets you near their face with sharp objects you're such a total loser" glare. This ticks Jim off so much that he asks Dr. Hernandez to remove me from the room.

I say, "What? I haven't opened my mouth."

ABC quickly says, "If Wynn has to leave the room then so does Jasper."

Dr. Hernandez says she thinks this would be an excellent time for both ABC and Jim to try therapy without their extended family present. She asks, "Do you both think we could try this without Jasper and Wynn?"

I look at ABC and say, "You know what Jasper and I can go into the waiting room. If you need me just yell and I'll come back in."

Jasper gives Jim big puppy dog eyes and says, "Same goes for me Jim Jim. I totes agree."

"Wow," I say, "Jim Jim. Now that's just adorable. Sorry," I say looking at Jasper, "I meant adorbs."

ABC smiles and Jim Jim says, "Get out. Get out now!"

As I'm walking out the door I look at Dr. Hernandez and say, "Forget about this co-parenting plan. You really need to work on his temper."

In the waiting room I take out my phone to play Scrabble, which I'm amazing at, in case you're curious. As I'm getting a triple word score I notice Jasper staring at me. I sigh and ask, "What is it Jasper?"

"You know Wynn," he says, "you could be a beautiful woman if..."

When he got to the "if", I interrupt him and say, "Stop, just stop. I know where you're going and it won't work. I'm a triple threat when it comes to trying to sell me anything. I'm the three C's - cheap, confident, and comfortable."

"Sers what do you mean by that? He asks.

"Jasper, if you and I are going to have a conversation I have to insist that you talk in full words. I'm not going to go all crazy and tax your brain by insisting you use full sentences, but actually say the word seriously, not just sers."

"Alright bitchy britches, I'll talk in complete words." He says while applying lip balm "Geesh. Now, explain these three C's to me."

127

"Okay." I yawn as I put my phone in my purse and say, "Let's start with the first C - I'm cheap. Brace yourself Jasper. I buy my skin care line at Costco with - - if I were you I'd put my head between my knees because it's going to make you light headed when I say this. Are you ready?"

Jasper, following my orders says, "I guess so."

"I buy Oil of Olay at Costco with a coupon."

Poor Jasper. I have to tell him to take deep, cleansing breaths. He looks pale. "Are you okay if I go on?"

"Yeah, I think so," he gasps. "It's the Oil of Olay that knocked the wind right out of me."

"Hang in there," I say encouragingly. The second C is confidence. You might look at me and think, 'What does this woman who needs to lose a few pounds and drives a minivan have to be confident about?' Well, let me answer that for you. I consider myself well loved by people who don't care if I have smile lines or a brow furrow."

"Okay, okay, I get that, but what about comfortable? That doesn't make sense?"

"Comfortable means I'm a woman who likes herself. I like that I can make myself laugh and I think I'm a decent wife, mother and friend. Don't you get it? I'm comfortable with who I am, no moisturizer harvested from the glands of sea urchins off the Almafi coast are needed to make me feel that way."

Jasper slowly sits upright in his chair and says, "I'm glad not many women have your three C's. It would really slow down business."

"Oh Jasper, a lot of women feel the way I do. For the most part females, particularly mothers, are a practical bunch. You only see the terminally scared at your day spa."

"Terminally scared?"

"You know scared of getting old or of change, any kind of change"

"You're right about that," he says while fluffing his hair, "which reminds me. I've been meaning to tell you that a group of women really hate you."

"Let me see, are their names Jacardia, Liz, Muchy, I mean Jen, and Caroline?

"Yes!" Jasper answers back sounding surprised that I nailed it.

"Were they all at the day spa today?"

"Yes, they were doing the Girls Day Out package.

"Besides bad mouthing me did you hear anything else they were talking about?"

"Lord woman, I heard all kinds of stuff. I was doing their caviar facials with a diamond tip exfoliation treatment and there's something about doing a buff and shine that just makes the girls talk and talk"

"Did they mention something called the Majesty Club or a principal?"

"They totes did, sorry I meant totally did, but I'm not going to tell you a word they said," Jasper is now grinning at me with an "I know something you don't know" smile.

"Is there some kind of day spa client privilege covenant that prevents you from spilling your guts, because your little foot that keeps on tapping lets me know that you really want to tell me."

"I'll tell you, but I'll need a favor."

"I'm listening."

"Next weekend is Jim's with his sons, but I want to go to a wine festival up at the lake. Can you please talk ABC into switching weekends with Jim?"

"I can try, but that's asking a lot." I pause for a couple seconds and act like his request is going to be hard to pull off and then say, "Okay, I can do better than try, I'll do it. You'll get your wine weekend."

Jasper claps his hands and says, "Yeah, Pinot Grigio here I come!"

I'm totally playing Jasper because I know ABC is always thrilled to have her boys with her as much as possible and gets very lonely when they're with their dad every other weekend. I don't tell Jasper that instead I act like I'm going to have to beg ABC to agree.

"It's your turn now," I tell him. "Spill it. Tell me everything they said."

Jasper grins, moves closer to me and says, "Girl, I know stuff that is going to rock that three C world of yours."

Week Four of the School Year

Depression Sets In

The news from Jasper was equal parts infuriating and intriguing. It took me a full week to process and more importantly, confirm, as best I could, everything he told me. If you add in what my Grace discovered during her play date with Windsor you have "situation critical." I have yet to share my findings with anyone. I'm still too shocked and depressed. This depression is much worse than the time I accidently read a *More* magazine (which I avoid, at all costs, due to their mission statement: Frightening women over forty about the aging process one Juvederm and Radiesse ad at a time) at the dentist office and discovered the best middle age has to offer is a field of stubborn chin hairs, that get so long they may curl and with your diminishing forty something vision you won't notice them until they become entangled in your low carb, whole wheat pasta.

My current, much worse, depression required a three part pick me up. First, I went on-line to various mother/parenting websites and posted ridiculous things in their mom conservation forums like, "I have two daughters ages three and five. The older one looks just like my mother-in-law which means she's not pretty at all. I'm hoping it's just a phase. Is it wrong that sometimes I don't think I love her as much as my unbelievably beautiful three-year-old who everyone says looks just like me?" I can't begin to explain how much fun it is to ignite this mom-on-mom shit storm. The name-calling, the threats - - it's delicious, non-caloric fun.

Next up I visited the mall where I attempted to regain some happiness by being a high functioning dumb ass. The food court was my starting line. I get a

131

Diet Coke, crushed ice, extra foam with twist of lime. After that, holding my Diet Coke (much like the Statue of Liberty is brandishing her freedom torch), I walked into the Louis Vuitton store and got escorted out by security. This, always, always brings me joy and laughter.

Louis Vuitton will not let you into their store if you have a drink. Correction, they will not let you enter their sanctuary of overpriced, over logoed leather goods if you have a drink from McDonalds. I've noticed all Starbucks beverages are allowed, even the drinks with whipped cream. I enjoyed entering Louis Vuitton with my Micky D's cup and observing the gasps from the sales clerk and the immediate call to security. I then start smiling when a conversation ensues with the security team and usually two sales clerks or, if I'm really lucky the store manager about why I can't have a McDonald's cup in the store. "I, would get it," I say, "if you had a zero tolerance for all beverages, but why is my Diet Coke from McDonalds, with a lid, I might add, so offensive?"

This line of reasoning baffles them. As they ponder this, I add, "And if you're so anti fast food why is your store located right next to the food court? Seriously, it smells Auntie Anne's Pretzels in here. I half expected you to be rolling dough on the counter. Those cylinder shaped purses over there could do double duty as rolling pins."

You can hear the audible intake of breath as the sales associate that looks like a former Pussy Cat Doll who washed her face and put a blouse from J Crew says, "Are you talking about the Papillon City Bag with the Yayoi Kosama's monogram in pumpkin as a rolling pin? That's, that's criminal. It's a $2,000 handbag!"

"Well, for two grand it's a good thing it's a multi-tasker." I say with authority.

This flusters them enough they offer to dispose of my Diet Coke for me and then and only then will I be allowed to browse in their store. This is when the fun really starts. I have to gently explain to them that my Diet Coke is fresh and has the perfect ice to soda ratio. "No way," I say, "am I going to toss out a Diet Coke this tasty."

The fact that I would chose my Diet Coke over the chance to go deep into their inner sanctum of purses, wallets and scarves unsettles them so completely that the security guard is instructed to forcibly escort me and my Diet Coke from the store. Good times.

Next in my effort to elevate my mood, I proceeded to the Lancome kiosk at Macy's. I lie to all three of the lab coat wearing women working behind the counter by telling them I'm 15 years older than I really am. This makes them ooh and ahh about how amazing I look. I know pretending to be a decade and half older than you really are to get compliments is desperate, but I was desperately depressed and it beats eating half a sheet cake. Plus, I needed some new mascara.

If I could confide in my friends I would feel better, but I'm afraid. ABC will go ballistic. Kelly will weep. I mean it, this news will bring her to tears and Nikki well, she'll get nervous and fidget which causes her lips to pout, which only makes her more gorgeous. Adding to my stress is I've received zero communications from the Roomba. Not one snippet of conversation has been sent to my son's computer. I hate to say this and it hurts me deeply as a mother to even entertain this possibility, but, (sigh) perhaps I over estimated my son's

133

skills. It's been over a week since the Roomba was placed in the principal's office. I've seen Jacardia up at school and according to my daughter a portion of the teacher's workroom has been converted into an office for the blonde one. You can bet I'll be taking a peek at that today which means there is one more thing to add to my To Do list. At the top - Roomba troubleshooting. This morning it's time to have a heart-to-heart with my son over his Honey Nut Cheerios. Fortunately, my husband is already at work and my daughter is still upstairs getting dressed so it's permission to talk freely time at the breakfast table.

As I'm pouring Clay some orange juice, I ever so gently, ask him about the possibility of the Roomba being, well, an experiment that didn't pan out. "Honey," I say, "about the Roomba is there just the smallest of chances it had a technical malfunction? I'm not saying you did anything wrong, but maybe something wasn't hooked up right."

"Mom," my son answers back like a teacher talking down to a classroom of students who all bombed their spelling test, "the Roomba was fully operational when it left this house. Did you ever consider that your friend ABC, not the most tech savvy or coordinated, knocked something lose or worse dropped it?"

"Okay, wee pompous one, dial down the tone. ABC and I aren't idiots. As for ABC she did not drop the Roomba. If she had she would have told me as in, 'Oh no I can't believe I dropped the Roomba!' But, we did move it from my Whole Foods grocery bag to her Spider Man backpack and she did put on the backpack and jog into the school. Would that have caused something to come loose?"

"Maybe," he says while shoving a big spoonful of cereal in his mouth. "We'll need to do some troubleshooting."

"Like what kind of troubleshooting?"

"We need to get someone to open up the back of the Roomba and make sure primarily that the battery is in place. It might have come just loose enough so it's not making a connection."

"Are you saying someone needs to sneak the Roomba out of the principal's office?"

"No, not at all. I'm saying someone needs to sneak into Mr. Parrish's office to do a little tech check."

"Yeah," I say while eating Cheerios out of the box, "I don't see that happening. I think the Roomba surveillance plan is now officially DOA."

That's when I head the pitter patter of pink tennis shoe feet and my daughter yell, "I'll do it and I already know how to get into the principal's office."

Great, super-ears strikes again. Before Grace can even get started on sharing with us her idea I shut her down. "No, nope, not going to happen. Don't say another word."

"But Mooooom," she wails, "it would be so easy."

"I don't care. It's totally unacceptable."

Clay chimes in with, "Come on Mom, at least you can let her tell us her plan. It's not like we don't have to listen to your schemes all the time."

I give Clay the evil eye for that comment and say, "Okay, Grace tell us what you were thinking," only because she looks like she's going to wet her pants if I don't let her talk.

She smiles really big and looks so cute, (I put her hair in pigtails this morning. Really, is there any cuter look for a girl?) that I want to pull her into my lap and give her cuddle kisses, but I restrain myself and let her talk as I take my hand out of the Cheerio box so I can pour some cereal into a bowl for her.

"All I would need to do is pretend to hurt myself on the playground during recess and ask to go to the nurse's office. I'm thinking a twisted ankle, that's always good for an ice pack. After I get the ice pack, I could sort of sneak into the principal's office, find the Roomba and see if the battery is shoved in the right way. That's all it needs, right Clay, for the battery to be shoved in?"

Clay answers with a mouth full of cereal, "Sort of something like that."

I quickly chime in, "Grace, sweetie, it's a very good plan, but I can't let you do it. It's not nice to fake an injury. You would be lying and what if the principal is in his office or worse what if you get caught in his office? "

"Duh, Mom, third grade recess is during fourth grade lunch. Mr. Parrish is always in the cafeteria during fourth grade lunch because the fourth graders are so bad. I heard my teacher tell another teacher that the fourth graders are the worst class in the whole, entire school!"

I'm thinking of all the fourth grade kids I know and kind of agreeing with the teacher's assessment of them which means I missed my chance to redirect the conversation into a more appropriate topic like, "Hey kids what do you think you want to be for Halloween?" Giving Grace the opportunity to continue full steam ahead.

"This means that I can go into Mr. Parrish's office and make sure the Roomba is working with no one seeing me. Oh and in case you're wondering how I know all about the Roomba. Clay's a show off and he told me how he built it. I also know the battery is on the back and all I have to do is make sure its connectors are hitting the connecty things"

"Clay! I'm very disappointed in your big mouth and Grace no, you are not doing anything. The Roomba discussion is officially over. Now, what do you kids think you want to be for Halloween?"

That conversation lasted until I got each of them dropped off at school. Clay wants to be Dr. Who and Grace is thinking Minnie Mouse. Of course, all of this could change by the time I pick them up from school in seven hours. When I get back home, I walk my two dogs Oreo and Chips Ahoy. It gives me a chance to wave at all the retired neighbors I see outside raking their leaves knowing as they wave back at me they're wondering when I'm going to rake my leaves. "Later, neighbors, much later," I say to myself. "They're leaves not Agent Orange." After I have happy dogs I take a quick shower. As my hair air dries I write up a Q and A I did for a company about their new CFO, email that off and then get dressed. I've got a secret Fall Festival meeting to attend.

Shh, It's a Secret Meeting

The confidential Fall Festival meeting is at my Parent Patrol buddy Heather Farro's house. Heather is chairperson of the Festival and this year the committee has taken to having clandestine conferences to avoid interacting with our illustrious PTA board of Jacardia, Murchy, Liz and Caroline. (Kelly as treasurer is on the board, but she doesn't count because she's not an ass.) The festival, as a fundraiser for the school and put on by volunteers, falls under the jurisdiction of the PTA. This means technically the foul foursome is "in charge" and Heather as chair of the fundraiser, reports to them. As Jasper would say this is, "totes stup" (totally stupid). To sidestep any of their interference and questionable suggestions, like Jacardia thinking a makeover booth for the cosmetically challenged would be fab and "give the ugly mothers something to do" or Murchy insisting that a prayer booth set up at a public elementary school would be "so righteous," we began holding secret meetings in June. It's amazing what you can get done when you have a room full of worker bees and zero Queen bees.

The Fall Festival is only two weeks away and Heather has done an outstanding job as chairperson. Today she has all of us meeting in her back yard which is gorgeous and an awesome advertisement for her landscaping company. The yard has it all: an expansive deck, a water feature, a tall stone fireplace that is a work of art, towering maple trees with their leaves just beginning to turn and pots and urns overflowing with pansies and crysthanamums. After oohing and aahing over Heather's amazing yard, all ten committee members get comfy in her teak lawn chairs that you can tell (unlike my outdoor furniture) is not from the Better

Homes and Garden Collection at Walmart. I'm feeling weird. ABC, Kelly and Nikki are all at the meeting and I want to take them over by the Koi pond and blurt out everything I've recently discovered, but I can't, not yet. My goal is tell them what I know and then immediately present my plan of action. The problem is I don't have a plan. ABC can tell something is wrong.

"Hey, what's up with you? You're quiet."

"Nothing. I'm just tired."

"Are you sure? She asks like she doesn't believe me.

"I promise that's all. I'm just worn out."

Before I can say anything more, Heather starts the meeting. Everyone there is in charge of some aspect of the Festival and Heather asks for updates from each of us. Croc Mom (wearing a camo Croc) raises her hand to go first and gives us a Fortune 500 worthy rundown of the rental logistics. Kelly, as PTA treasurer briefs us on the ticket sales. ABC, who's in charge of all of the game stations takes four-seconds to say, "It's all good. No problems."

Nikki takes about the same about of time to update us on the face painting and costume booths which means, now it's my turn to report on the "Festival Treat" stations otherwise known as the junk food booths. Being committee chair of the junk food is a job I take very seriously. I especially love the cotton candy booth. It takes a special person to work in close quarters with cotton candy. Your lungs have to be able to tolerate working in a sugar cloud for six hours and you've got to have the moves down to take what is essentially the world's longest Tampax applicator and twirl wads of cotton candy around it. It's the twirling that stumps

139

most people. I tell them it's all in the wrist, but I guess it's like anything else, practice makes perfect and I've had ample hands on experience with cotton candy. I give my report on where we stand on renting the equipment and supplies for the cotton candy, corn dogs, churros and snow cones stations and then excitedly share I've scored a deep fried Twinkie booth. Even better, it uses 100% organic vegetable oil as the fryer grease.

"It took me a bunch of Google searches and two visits to the State Fair to get all this worked out, but I'm thrilled to tell you semi-organic, deep fried, limited edition, Twinkies will be added to the junk food station!"

A couple of moms start clapping and one mom, whom I call, TBTT, it stands for (Too Busy To Tinkle) raises her hand.

Oh no, I think, here it comes, a protest about the nutritional content of the deep fried Twinkie from, of course, the busiest women in the burbs. Well, let me backtrack a bit. TBTT validates her self-worth by thinking she is the most extraordinarily busiest Mom in the history of parenting which results in her never having time to go to the bathroom. Every conversation I've ever had with her starts with some version of, "Oh my God! I'm about to wet my pants. I've been so busy I haven't peed since 6:15 this morning. I've had four coffees, three meetings and no time to go potty."

I've called her out on this a few times. I mentioned how it's not a good thing to ignore nature's call and even that it's a tad awkward to start every conversation with an over share of your bodily functions, but she continues to ignore my advice.

"Yes, Meredith (TBTT's real name)" I say. "Do you have a concern about the Twinkies?"

"I just don't get how they're organic. They're still Twinkies, right? And hello, we're going to get a ton of complaints about adding more junk to the junk food stations. I thought it was part of a the PTA's five-year plan to phase out all unhealthy food at every Parent Teacher Association sanctioned event."

I look at Heather and ABC, roll my eyes and say, "Meredith, you are, of course, right. The Twinkies are still crap. The only thing organic is the oil they will be deep fried in, but because we'll have a large sign that says, 'Limited Edition Deep Fried Twinkies in Organic Oil' I will bet you a 12 pack of three ply toilet paper that the Twinkie booth, at five bucks a Twinkie, will be the biggest money maker at the Festival."

Heather adds, "If you remember, Meredith, three years ago we tried having only healthy food booths. Let's see, I think we did water, apple and carrot stick stations and the Festival didn't make as much money. The junk food is a draw. It brings out families that don't even go to our school."

Kelly jumps in with, "And don't forget, there is the Farmers Market section of the Festival where you can buy fruits and vegetables. Who doesn't love roasted red pepper hummus and zucchini sticks?"

"Relax Meredith," I say. "It's going to be fine. It's a festival not a health fair."

"Okay, but I'm telling you get ready for moms going off, big time, about adding another junk food booth. When they do, I'll tell them to go directly to you Wynn." TBTT says with a self-satisfied smile.

141

"I'll look forward to it because I can't wait to tell them if they don't want their kids to eat a deep fried Twinkie then don't buy them one! There, the problem of their kids eating nutritionally flawed food is instantly solved. Call me a miracle worker."

"Whatever." TBTT says and then asks Heather, "Where's your bathroom? I had to go pee like three hours ago and haven't had time."

Heather answers, "Past the kitchen and right next to the laundry room."

As Meredith is running to the bathroom, Heather updates the rest of the committee on the Fall Festival Talent Show. The talent show takes place in the evening after the Festival in the cafetorium. Up until three years ago, it was an event that featured students singing, dancing, telling jokes, maybe some double Dutch jump roping and usually you could count on at least one dramatic reading of *Green Eggs and Ham*. This mosh pit of talent was lovingly overseen by the music teacher who, in her genius, limited each "act" to two minutes or less, which meant parents could be in and out in under two hours. When the music teacher retired, Jacardia and company moved in on the talent show like bed bugs setting up camp at an airport Holiday Inn Express. It was bye-bye to adorable second graders singing "*My Favorite Things*" from *The Sound of Music* and hello to PTA moms in rhinestone clad costumes, that barely cover their reproductive bits, doing "Spring Creek Elementary Presents: Dancing with the Stars."

Oh, for sure, there was protest aplenty about this, but Jacardia was ready. She explained that by taking the talent show and "re-imagining" it as Dancing with the Stars it became another fundraiser for the school. The kiddie talent show was

142

free. Tickets to see moms doing an eager beaver straddle in an outfit rejected by the Las Vegas Show Girls Guild for excessive vulgarity are sixty bucks apiece. The show sells out every year.

What is it that has turned this current generation of mothers into boa constrictors? We take any traditional kid-centric activity, like a talent show, swallow it whole and then regurgitate it into being all about us. Look at kids' birthday parties. They used to be pin-the-tail-on-the-donkey, low-key affairs. Now, it's Battle of the Best Birthday Party Moms.

The Festival committee, thank God, has zero to do with the talent show, but Heather asks for volunteers to work that night. "I know the whole Dancing with the Stars thing is not," she stops in mid-sentence, looks at all of us and says, "anyone's cup of tea, but I've gotten a request from the PTA board to help round up some helpers for the evening."

Nikki raises her hand and asks, "What would we have to do? Is it working the concessions or something?"

Heather says, "There's that and they need help backstage with costumes and quick changes. Liz Derby gave me a list. I'll pass it around and please, if you can spare the time, sign-up. Liz and Jacardia are tag teaming me with phone calls and texts. I'm going to be forced to change my cell phone number if they don't stop."

Heather was high if she thought that I, after overseeing all the junk food booths, and most likely covered head-to-toe in cotton candy sugar and deep fried Twinkie batter, was then going to volunteer to help the Dancing with the Stars skank squad that evening. Lord, I'd barely have time lick the sugar off. As the

143

sign-up sheet is going around, Nikki and Kelly laugh when it gets to me. Kelly jokes, "Don't tell me you're going to miss out on the opportunity to bond with Jacardi and her fellow dancers?"

I look at the sheet, start to laugh and then I get an idea. A brilliant idea, stunning, in its simplicity. Before I even have a chance to fully appreciate all this idea has to offer, my cell phone rings. It's the elementary school. Grace has hurt her ankle on the playground. I'm thinking, "Oh no, she didn't!" and excuse myself from the meeting to see what my eight-year-old has gotten herself into.

Faker

As I'm driving to the school, I'm getting angrier by the second at my daughter. What part of "the Roomba plan is dead" did she not understand? She's in a whole bunch of trouble this time. When I get to the nurses office Grace is attempting to look like she's in pain. When she sees me, she groans. Oh my God, is that a tear? When did she master crying on command? Before I can say anything, she moans again and says, "Mom, I think I need to go to Urgent Care and get an x-ray."

I give her a look that says equal parts "Don't push your luck" and "You're in really, really, big trouble." Nurse Cannon, after showing me her engagement ring, suggests I take her home and keep her leg elevated and iced.

"I don't think it's broken, but keep an eye on it and don't let Grace apply pressure to her left foot. She tried to walk earlier and as she was going down the hall she fell. I found her crawling on the floor in the principal's office. The poor thing said she was looking for a chair so she could use it to pull herself up."

"Really," I say. "You found her in the principal's office?"

"Yes, I told her she should have called for help, but she said she didn't want to bother anyone. What a sweetheart Grace is."

Grace gives Nurse Cannon a big smile as I roll my eyes. "Okay, Grace let's get you home. Do you need me to carry you to the car?"

145

"No, I think if I just lean on you and hop I'll be okay," she says while pretend sniffling.

I help Grace stand up and wrap my arm around her waist as she begins hopping out of the office.

"You, young lady," I whisper, "are in a heap of trouble."

"I've already figured that out. My plan was perfect right until Nurse Cannon saw me in the principal's office. Before you start yelling at me, do you want to take a peek at Mrs. Monroe's new office?"

Of course I want to see what Jacardia's newest lair looks like, but I'm about to start scolding my daughter. The pull of snooping is just too strong - immediate and excessive scolding is put on hold to see what the Super Witch is up too.

"Can you hop there?" I ask.

"Why do I still have to hop? We're out of the nurses' office."

"Because you, great big faker, will hop yourself right out of this school all the way to my car. Consider it part of your punishment."

"But I'm getting tired of hopping on the same leg."

"Too bad. Now, where's Mrs. Monroe's new office?"

"Remember, I told you she took part of the teacher's workroom over and made it all fancy."

"It's fancy? I ask in disbelief. "Hop faster! I've got to see this."

"Okay, okay, slow down," Grace whines as I turn my walk into a sprint.

As we both hop/jog into the teachers' workroom I see nothing unusual. There are a couple of copiers, shelves with stacks of paper, crayons, glue-sticks and an automatic stapler that looks like, in a pinch, you could use it to kill someone. I look at Grace and say, "Where's the fancy?"

"Over there, Mom, behind the shelves."

"How do you know so much about the teachers workroom? You're not going places you're not supposed to are you?" I ask Grace worried that instead of recess she's roaming the halls for Intel.

"Sometimes a teacher will ask for two volunteers to go the workroom and pick up something a mom is copying for her."

"That's alright then," I say relieved as I'm walking behind the shelves. I know I've hit the land of Jacardia when I see an ocelot rug. I'm sure it's a carpet remnant from her closet. Jacardia has managed to turn what used to be a rather large storage area into Pottery Barn Tramp. Besides the rug, she has a white desk with an office chair covered in a cheetah throw. On the desk are various pictures of Jacardia in zebra frames and she's somehow managed to hang up two mirrors and drag in a lamp with a bedazzled shade. Other than the inappropriateness of it all I don't see anything nefarious going on. No papers to look at, no laptop, no scribbles on a tiger print post it, nothing that says uh oh. I glance at Grace and say, "I'm glad I got to see this, but it's time to get you home so start hopping."

When we get in the car I give Grace the lecture she's been expecting - the whole no means no - thing. I stress that at eight or eighty, she is never ever allowed to call an audible on the law or laws I have laid down. She seems sorry although, I have no doubt she is probably more sorry she got caught or didn't get the chance to fiddle with the Roomba. When we get home, I send her up to her room to await further punishment. I need some alone time. I want to fully explore the possibilities of the idea that came to me when I was at Heather's house. Just as I'm pouring myself a fresh Diet Coke to aid me in my pondering the phone rings. It's my husband with a request. He wants the kids and me to spend the afternoon picking up leaves.

"Is there a leaf disposal emergency I don't know about?" I ask him. "Did someone complain? Who picks up leaves on a weekday unless you're retired?"

"No, no and I don't know, but there are a lot of leaves in our yard and I think it would be the neighborly thing to do, a sign of yard solidarity, for my family to be seen raking and bagging leaves."

I was going to fight him on his request, but then I thought raking leaves would be a good punishment for Grace so I say, "Okay, I'll get the kids on it right after school. We'll be leaf bagging machines. No problem."

"Okay, what's going on?" My husband asks concerned. "That was way too easy."

"Nothing, I swear. Just bring a pizza home for dinner to reward us for our raking abilities."

"Alright, rake well. I'll be home about six."

I get off the phone, pat myself on the back for figuring out a punishment for Grace and not having to make dinner tonight then look at the clock and realize it's almost time to pick up Clay from school.

Coming Attractions

As soon as Clay gets in the car I share the news that leaf raking will begin right after he has a snack. Grace, as a punishment will be getting the dreaded rake duty. Clay will be mowing, mulching and bagging the leaves, and I will be using the leaf sucker-up thing to assist in getting the leaves out of the hard-to-reach places. Clay complains immediately, "Why do I have to be punished and made to do yard work on a school day, when I didn't do anything wrong?"

"Pipe down Clay," I say. "It's family bonding. There are Hallmark cards about leaf raking."

"Are they about hating your family and nature? Because I'd buy that card."

I pretend I didn't hear that smart-ass comment and turn the radio on NPR to give both kids something new to bitch about. Amid all the grousing and clever maneuvers to get out of lawn work I've stayed on schedule and now have both kids in the yard doing chores. Clay is mowing, Grace is raking, and I've strapped on the Ultra Yard Vac Turbo Edition 3-in-1 blower, vacuum and leaf shredder. The Yard Vac is the answer to my prayer. It's so loud I can't hear Grace complaining. The noise is also helping me meditate on the idea I had at Heather's. The only problem is the leaf sucker-upper is a little unwieldy and as the bag attached to it fills with leaves it gets heavy. I'm having to balance it a bit between my legs to maintain optimum control of the vacuum nozzle.

After about ten minutes of this I start feeling funny, funny-good, like really good. My face is getting flushed and it's not from exertion. I look down and notice my grip on the Ultra Yard Vac has slipped a tad and its 1.2 horsepower, vibrating motor is lounging in my sweet spot. I know I should move it, but I can't, not yet. Wait for it. Oh God, no, there's a neighbor. Please don't come over here neighbor. I can't even lift my hand to wave. It would require me to move the Yard Vac and that's a no can do. This bad boy isn't going anywhere just yet. I'm keeping my hand down and ignoring the neighbor. I surreptitiously look around. My kids are in the backyard. That's all I need to see to give myself permission to let go. Oh-My-God, for richer, for poorer, in sickness and in health, to love and to cherish; from this day forward until death do us part I pledge thee to the Ultra Yard Vac. I'm shaken out of my post-coital Yard Vac euphoria by my husband Sam. He's home early and is holding a large pizza. I think he saw me cheating on him with the 3-in-1.

Sam, staring at me, says, "Are you okay?"

"Yes, I'm perfectly fine," I say curtly. "How long have you been standing there?"

"Long enough. What's up with you and the leaf blower?"

"What do you mean what's up?"

"It just looked like you were really enjoying doing yard work, that's all I'm saying."

"For your information, I was enjoying tidying up the yard."

He smiles at me, looks at the 3-in-1 and says, "Yeah, with your new boyfriend" and then runs away from me laughing as I try to hit him with the plastic leaf nozzle. Whatever I'm sure I'm not the first woman to achieve a certain level of satisfaction from Ultra Yard Vac Turbo Edition. Like it's my fault a company designed a yard tool with a motor that based on your height, may become connected to your crotch. No wonder I see so many women using their leaf blowers. As I'm putting away my yard vibrator I hear Clay yell, "Mom, the Roomba transmitted. I've got five minutes of video on my computer!"

I scream, "Coming!" (and get embarrassed about my poor word choice because of well, you know) drop the yard vibrator on the floor of the garage and run inside and upstairs to Clay's room. Before I can even see the Roomba transmission my husband comes into the room and says, "When do you want to eat? The pizza is going to get cold."

"In a minute, Honey. Clay wants to show me a project he's working on."

"Okay, great. Let's see it Clay."

Crap. Sam doesn't need to see this. It will set him off big time and my argument that yes, I know it's illegal, but it's for the greater good of mankind will only tick him off more. I look at Clay. Clay looks at me, gives me a goofy raised eyebrow and says, "Dad, I don't want you to see the project just yet. I'm still working on it and I want it to be perfect when I officially unveil it."

Oh, he's smooth, that son of mine, maybe too smooth. And of course the guilt I'm feeling for sanctioning my child to lie to his dad is crushing my chest. (Sort of. By that I mean it's called a marriage not truth serum).

My husband laughs and says to our son, "Very well done, Clay. But, I'm not an idiot. I know your mother thinks she's the 007 of the suburbs and you're her

Q. Just remember I'm M. The boss. You two have five minutes then dinner is served."

I feel like Clay and I both dodged a bullet, but I'm a little ticked off my husband thinks he's the boss. For sure, he has many fine leadership qualities, but I always thought I was the boss. I'm tempted to follow him down to the kitchen and discuss this, but then I hear Jacardia's voice.

"Clay, you did it! It works," I say excitedly.

"No I did it," Grace says triumphantly, walking into the room. "I snuck in the principal's office, found the Roomba and pushed the battery back in. If it weren't for me you would have nothing. A great big zero"

Clay gives his little sister a high five and says, "Good job. Right now I can honestly say I've found a reason for your existence on earth. Now get out of my room."

"Mom, do I have to?"

"Yes, you do. Go help your dad set the table. And it doesn't matter that you were a Roomba troubleshooter you still disobeyed me. You got that?"

"Uh huh and I'm sorry, but it was still exciting," she says as she runs out of her brother's room before I can continue scolding her.

"Mom, are you ready to hear it now? Clay asks.

"Yes, but I'm thinking maybe you need to leave the room. There could be stuff they say I don't want you to hear."

"Whatever," he sighs, "although, I don't think it's fair I did all the technical work and now I'm getting kicked out of my own room."

"You'll get over it. Now scoot."

As soon as Clay is out of his room I press the button he showed me that would play the Roomba video. The sound quality is excellent, but the video stinks. All I see are feet. "Clay, Clay," I shout, "come back in here for a second."

"You don't have to yell Mom. I'm right outside my door. What is it?"

"All I see are feet. What's up with that?"

"Mom, it's a Roomba - a vacuum that is like an inch off the ground. What do you think you would see? I didn't build it to have a periscope with a camera. Don't you think that would have raised some suspicions - a Roomba with a periscope?"

"Sorry," I say. "Now show me how to rewind on your computer and get out again."

Clay does as he's told and I start the recording over. For the first couple of minutes Jacardia is flirting with the principal. She's telling him how much she likes his blazer, how it brings out the blue in his eyes. Then she abandons flirting and moves into seductress mode. I can tell because her voice has gone all breathy and I notice Jacardia's and Mr. Parrish's feet are getting closer together. It looks like they're standing toe-to-toe.

Jacardia coos and says, "It would make my life so much easier if you could do me a little, itty, bitty favor. You know how I'm helping you so much by taking care of the crazy parents and their silly demands on your time so you can focus on all the really important - us? Well, if you would share that school district computer password of yours I could help even more. Think of me as your assistant. Your really sexy assistant. I could do your data entry stuff and it would give us a chance to work together even more, like a whole lot more. Why don't you show me how much you would really love that?"

Stupid Roomba. Now, I don't see any freaking feet, but I'm still hearing talking and heavy male breathing. Where are their feet? What's happened? "Clay," I yell, "why would I not be seeing feet, but still be getting video of the floor?"

"I dunno Mom maybe they're sitting on a desk or something."

Or I think in horror, laying on a desk. The principal is horizontal on his desk with Jacardia. Holy Candy Corn Oreos! After about 45 seconds the heavy breathing stops and the principal says, "My password is Jacardia1 and you have to keep it secret that I gave it to you. I could lose my job if anyone finds out."

I again see feet, but only Jacardia's. "Oh sweetums don't worry. I've got that big, strong back of yours," she whispers. I see and hear her feet leave and the Roomba transmission ends.

I'm stunned. I feel like I could be stroking out. There's too much to process. Jacardia and the principal doing the afternoon delight or at least an office make-out session on a desk in a freaking elementary school! The fact that my clever, disobedient daughter fixed the Roomba and almost evaded capture on what I will now and forever call D Day. The pride of ownership I feel in my son for rigging a Roomba into a mobile surveillance drone. Fear for myself if I get

155

caught orchestrating and possessing an illegally taped conversation. All of this is nothing compared to the rage that is making my left arm go numb and causing me to lose consciousness as I'm thinking about Jacardia now being in possession of what is basically, the launch code to get in to every student's and teacher's personal records! It's like Lex Luthor getting ahold of a lifetime supply of Kryptonite.

Forget about dinner I need to check and make sure my pupils are evenly dilated, a sign that I'm not having a stroke, and then call an emergency meeting at the League of Justice, and by that I mean me, ABC, Kelly and Nikki all need to rendezvous at the AARP five star-rated Streamside Assisted Living Facility and Nursing Home.

Pain & Suffering

I had to wait exactly twenty-four hours before my friends could meet me at the nursing home. It was painful cooling my jets for that long, but logistics had to be worked out. Everyone needed to line up her spouse or parents for kid-watching duty and ABC had to score us a room at Streamside. She works at the nursing home as a speech pathologist and is beloved by the staff and residents. Things that usually get her in trouble, like her inability to censor her mouth, are appreciated at Streamside. The elderly residents love her because as one ninety year old gentleman told me, "When you get to be my age, there's nothing better than a gal who's a straight shooter and can curse like a sailor."

Because ABC is so highly thought of, she's been able to finagle us a room in the Streamside's assisted living section when the facility is at less-than-full occupancy. This is where we have our "Escape from Our Families" therapy sessions. It's way better than a Marriott Courtyard or Fairfield Inn. The room is like those super swanky birthing suites they have in the hospital maternity wards where they hide or disguise all the medical stuff. You've got two really plush beds that look normal, but have the hospital push button recline and lower features. Plus, there's a queen size pull-out sofa bed. The TV is huge (to help residents with macular degeneration issues) and who doesn't like a shower where you can sit down in a chair?

The best part is the food. Pot roast, mashed potatoes with brown gravy, green beans seasoned with bacon grease and sour cream yeast rolls with honey butter - all amazing. Then there are the pies. The coconut cream pie with what must be at least two inches of fluffy meringue topping, is 1940 County Fair blue-ribbon

157

worthy. It's like the chef at Streamside wants the residents to time travel back to their youth by cooking the food they grew up with.

We all meet in the Streamside assisted living suite #404 at exactly 5:30 pm. Everyone wants to know what's going on, but I suggest we go to the dining room (for the ambulatory residents) and eat first. Swiss steak with scalloped potatoes is on menu, and no matter how concerned I am about Jacardia and company, I wasn't going to let it affect my appetite. We all finish dinner in a hurry, get our slices of pie to go and head back to the suite. It's ABC who says, "So, out with it. What information, to quote your phone message, is, 'life altering?'"

I was hoping to eat my pie first, but everyone looks ready to find out what's gong on. So I take a big bite of coconut cream and say, "Well, in the past week I've discovered some information that has lead me to believe the PTA board, minus Kelly, of course, is about to release a covert shit storm on the school. Now before anyone says anything, I have some visual aids I need to get out."

I'm a firm believer in color-coded handouts and a poster board flowchart has never let me down. I stop talking, walk over to my overnight bag, grab the handouts and then remove a black Hefty trash bag I had put over the poster board. I lean the poster board on an IV tray and give the handouts to Nikki to pass around. As soon as ABC gets the handout she starts cursing (and they're the ones I really don't approve of - you know the gd and mf variety).

"ABC, save it till I get finished," I say. "It's gonna get worse."

She shuts up mid curse and I get started detailing my findings. I'm saving the "Jacardia + Principal = True Love 4 Ever" till the end.

In detail, I begin with what Jasper told me the night of ABC's family counseling session. Before ABC can jump it and say, "Why the hell would you believe that dumb ass?" I quickly add that trusting no one, I verified all the information to the best of my ability. Using the chest piece on the stethoscope as a pointer, I work my way down the poster board chart starting with embezzlement. This is when Kelly turns as white as Jacardia's hair.

"Jasper, the eavesdropping facialist to the criminally vain," I say, "overheard Jacardia, Murchy, Liz and Caroline brag about their 'free' spa day. He asked if they had all gotten gift certificates and this question, he said, made them all have a giggle fit. Jacardia explained that the PTA was 'picking up the tab' for their day of beauty. Jasper went in for the follow-up question while he was extracting (that would be popping to the non-facialist community) a big zit on Liz's forehead and commented how 'unusual' it was they were able to use PTA funds to pay for a spa day. Liz, according to Jasper winced as he stabbed her zit and then whimpered, 'Well, let's just say Michael's is paying for it.' Jasper, not being me, thought it meant some guy on the PTA (who was not one of their husbands) was footing their spa day. I, of course, knew instantly - they meant Michael's, the craft store. As we all know one of the largest expenditures any decent PTA has is to Michael's."

I look at Kelly and ask, "Isn't that right?"

"Yes," she says. "You've got moms hitting up the craft store for art supplies, paper, foam board, ribbon, etc. Michael's carries all sorts of stuff needed for any

PTA project or fundraiser and all the moms turn in their receipts to be reimbursed."

"Exactly what I thought," I say. "This lead me to ask Jasper how much, to the penny, their girls day out at the spa cost. I also asked him if he could look over the spa records and see how much each woman had spent there over the past four weeks. It cost me, but he did it."

"How much did it cost you?" ABC asks. "I can't believe the little twerp agreed to do anything for you without some form of cash incentive."

"Never mind about that right now, ABC, I've got it covered. Where was I? Oh yeah, once I had that information I went to Kelly and asked to see the PTA accounts payable spreadsheet. I must admit that I know it's handed out at every PTA meeting, but, up until now, I had never gone over it line item by line item. This is where I confirmed each Michael's receipt the four of them had turned in all matched exactly to their spa bills. It was a simple scheme to pull off. All they had to do was copy and paste the Michael's logo and then phony up a receipt with a total amount that covered their spa bill. They even got away with not matching the Michael's receipt paper because they submitted multiple receipts photocopied on a regular 8 1/2 x 11 piece of paper. I'm sure the only thing that stumped them was figuring out the sales tax."

ABC jumps off one of the hospital beds and snarls, "Are you telling me our kids have been selling fucking gift-wrap, fucking cookie dough and fucking magazine subscriptions to finance their fucking spa days?"

"Yes, but can you sit back down. There's more."

"How can there be more? I think that's enough. Isn't that enough? I don't think we need more," Nikki says looking worried that ABC might spontaneously combust.

"What? Do you want me to stop? Because I can stop right now." I am getting a little ticked that no one is acting like they want to hear the rest of what is a very well-researched report.

ABC sits down and says, "No, go ahead" and then asks if anyone packed liquor.

Nikki goes to her suitcase and takes out four mini bottles of what looks like airplane whiskey and hands one to ABC. They both chug it.

I notice Kelly hasn't said anything and looks mad at me, but that has to be wrong. I pick up the stethoscope and return to working my way down the flowchart.

"Now if you'll look at your handout, I'm moving on to the Majesty Club concern which is printed in the hot pink ink."

I thought it would make Kelly happy that I had followed up on her request to find out what's going on, but she won't even make eye contact with me. I'm sure it's because she's so upset about the bogus receipts. I continue to breakdown what I had discovered about Liz Derby's new mother/daughter invitation-only service club.

"Working off a tip from Jasper and some Intel from my daughter who after a play date with Windsor, discovered the time and location of a Majesty Club meeting, I disguised myself in my Halloween costume from last year. Remember, I was Dr. Chainsaw? I put on my XXL green surgical scrubs, shoved my hair in a surgical cap and wore my oversize lawn mowing sunglasses. You could barely see my face. I took my husband's more incognito car and tailed the mother daughter volunteer caravan of one Range Rover, one Escalade and one Porsche Cayenne.

Their first stop was the mall where their 'public service' was having their daughters go the American Girl store to have their dolls hair styled in an up-do. They then headed to Starbucks where the girls got venti double chocolate chip Frappuccinos and the moms got drinks with non-fat whatever (except Caroline who ordered her usual hot water with lemon). As their daughters ran - unsupervised, I might add, around the Starbucks, the moms had, what I'm thinking, was an impromptu meeting. They mulled over their criteria for admission into the Majesty Club. That list was less about what they wanted and more about what they didn't want. It included and I'm quoting: No fatties, point of note, the fatty comment extends to both mother and daughter. If either one is in Caroline's words, 'a chubbette' they're not to be admitted. Also on the list: no DIY'ers, no minivanners, no clearance rackers and no coupon whores.' So basically, they just don't want me. Thank you Lord."

Nikki, whose face has turned a deep red (that's nevertheless extremely becoming on her) says, "They're horrible, horrible women!"

"No argument from me on that, but I haven't gotten to the good part yet. They also discussed their master plan of using the Majesty Club to win the annual Community of Young Givers award."

162

I just dropped a bomb, so I'm glad to hear all three of them say, almost in unison, "Shit!"

The Community of Young Givers award is given by the school district to a student service group that exemplifies the spirit of volunteering. It is a ruthless and cutthroat competition. This is what happens when you start having kids log their community service hours. Gone are the days when families, scout groups, or religious organizations would quietly and without the whole "look at me" fanfare do volunteer work for the sole sake of giving back. Now, it's all about writing down and keeping track of every nanosecond you spend doing something for someone else because being a decent human being isn't its own reward. Parents want their kids to have the chance to win a prize for it.

The group who wins the Community of Young Givers award receives tons of publicity including being on the front page of the local newspaper and on billboards. The best thing is the all-expense paid trip to Hawaii (funded by a local bank, not the school district) to compete at the national level. Usually, high school aged kids win, but the judges (school administrators and the bank president) are suckers for younger kids doing community service. I can hear the "pint size role model" speech coming out of the school board president's mouth already. It seems that Jacardia, Liz, Caroline, Murchy and the other Majesty Moms have also figured that out. Each school's principal is allowed to nominate one group of students for the award. No doubt, Jacardia already has taken care of that.

"I'm telling you, the moms think they already have it the bag. Bikinis and getting the bank to pay for an 'on-site teacher' (which we know means babysitter so the moms can go off and get their tropical drunk on) were being discussed."

"But wait," asks Nikki. "Don't they have to do lots of community service? You can't fake that, can you?"

ABC answers with, "Yeah, you can. I'm sure the district checks the teenagers community service logs like forensic accountants going over a New Jersey mob boss's tax receipts, but since this is eight, nine and ten-year-old girls and their mothers, no one will check. They won't think to question the word of a mom. It's just like when Aleexiah Monroe wins the summer reading award ever year and we all know she for damn sure didn't read 131 books."

I continue. "And they did do some community service the day I tailed them. They dropped off a bag of sweaters at the public television station's Mr. Rogers' Sweater Drive. You should have seen them with their one, that's *uno*, grocery bag of sweaters. You would have thought it was filled with the cremated remains of Big Bird or something. Outside the TV station, the girls all took turns carrying the bag and the moms snapped tons of pictures of the girls with a banner that said, '*Majesty Girls Care about Our Community.*' It was nauseating. After they left, I went inside the station (minus the surgical cap and sunglasses) and asked the receptionist if could count the sweaters. She thought I was a creeper, but she let me. There was total of seven used kid's sweaters in the bag. There used to be eight, but Murchy's daughter Carrington, saw one of her sweaters in the bag, took it out and yelled "I don't want ugly people wearing my stuff!'"

I stop talking for a second for dramatic effect and because I need to catch my breath. I'm surprised when no one says anything. I thought for sure the ugly people comment would have at least set ABC off. I clear my throat and say, "If you consult your handout, you'll see we're now down to the last category: Jacardia and the principal. It's the purple ink section. For this segment, I have a multi-media presentation."

I take out my iPad, (where I have downloaded the Roomba video) and hand it to Nikki, I don't want ABC holding it, because I'm afraid after she sees what's on it, she'll throw the iPad across the room. It takes only a couple of seconds of watching the video before ABC jumps up and keeps repeating the world's worst swear word. Kelly's face freezes in such a way she looks like the guy in Edvard Munch's *The Scream* and Nikki's hands begin to shake. Their reaction is so swift I hardly have time to get ready for part two of my presentation - Retribution.

The plan I have masterminded is, I think, my best work to date. I've very pleased with myself and my heart is beating fast in my chest because I'm excited to share my Four Planks of Payback. I don't mean to brag, but this plan of mine could be bordering on genius. No, scratch that: it *is* genius. I hear Jacardia on the video saying "Oh Sweetums" which means it's about to end. I take a deep breath to prepare to launch into part two of my presentation. I've already flipped the poster board over, so as soon as ABC, Kelly and Nikki take their eyes off the iPad, they'll see the illustrated version of my Four Planks. I've used the professional series chisel-tip Sharpie's and my poster board work is stunning, easy-to-read and colorful. I have the stethoscope in my hand and I'm ready to start working my way down the poster board when Nikki blurts out, "I don't get it. What good will it do Jacardia to get into the files of the kids and teachers? And, yuck on her doing anything with the principal. He's old, like really old."

"It's all about power, Nikki. Information is power and Jacardia wants to dig through those files and find out everything she can. Think of what's in them: kids' IQ scores, notes from the counselor or district psychologist, teachers' salaries and performance reviews, even who's on the free and reduced lunch program. She would have been like a kid in a candy store."

ABC is so pissed, she looks like she wants to punch someone. She curses, paces, curses some more, sits back down and gives me a really angry look. I'm not being overly dramatic when I tell you it resembles a death ray. She asks, "What do you mean 'would have been?'"

"As soon as I saw this, I had Clay do something to make the password not work. He wrote some code that only let her access district files about the cafeteria, transportation and custodial supply orders. My goal was to let her get into the files, just not where she wanted to go. I didn't want to spook her and let her know someone was on to her. I just wanted to neutralize her."

Kelly looks up from the iPad with tears in her eyes. I swell up with pride thinking they're tears of gratitude. I did do some very fine detective work. She looks at me and says, "I think I hate you right now."

"Huh?" I say because Kelly is misdirecting her anger at me, when, of course, what she really needs to do is focus on my most excellent plan.

Nikki, rubbing Kelly's back, says, "I'm with Kelly. You've really screwed us over, Wynn."

"Okay, I'm so not getting where this anger is coming from," I say a little ticked off." "Is it 'kill the messenger?' because I'm the one that has been doing the hard core detective work for more than a week and I've got a plan - a really good plan."

ABC stands up and I'm thinking it's to come over to me to literally and figuratively have my back. But, no, ABC grabs her overnight tote and starts shoving her stuff in it. What the hell?

"Are you leaving, ABC?

"Yeah, I'm out of here."

That's all it took for Nikki and Kelly to both stand up and grab their bags. Kelly says, "We're all out of here."

"What's going on? Are you mad at me? Why would you be mad at me?"

Kelly looking like she wants to vigorously shake me says, "I can't speak for Nikki and ABC, but here's why I'm furious at you. You think you're better than me. Here's a news flash you're not!"

"Kelly, what are you talking about? I would never think that! You're on my top five list of the smartest people I know. What's going on here?"

I'm so confused, worried, hurt and a whole lot of angry that I'm sweating through my Target crew neck T-shirt. Why are my best friends turning on me? I don't get it. Good thing we're in a nursing home because I feel like I might need oxygen stat!

"What's going on," she says, "is this: by keeping all the bogus receipt crap to yourself, you've put me in a terrible position. I'm the treasurer, Wynn. I took the forged receipts Jacardia, Caroline, Murchy and Liz gave me and I reimbursed them. I could be culpable. I have a fiduciary responsibility to protect the PTA money and don't even get me started on the applicable provisions of the Sarbanes-Oxley Act. If this gets out it could seriously harm my reputation as a CPA and my business. You know, the thing that feeds my family and keeps a roof over our heads? You should have told me as soon as you found out. That should have been your very first thought. But no, you couldn't do that could you? You had to be the hero and come up with one of your schemes because you think you're all that."

Before I even have a chance to defend myself Nikki chimes in with, "Kelly's right. I thought we were all a team, but you do treat us like we're not as smart as you. I thought it was just me because you know I'm younger and all but I guess we all feel this way."

I'm speechless. I'm clutching the stethoscope to my chest as I stumble backwards so I can lean on the bed for support. I look at ABC, my best friend for thirteen years, and ask, "Do you feel this way too? Please tell me you don't feel this way."

"Shit, Wynn, why did you keep all this to yourself? You should have told us! I helped plant the Roomba in the principal's office. I thought we were in this together. Your problem is you're a fucking control freak."

"We're all control freaks!" I shout. "We're mothers. If we weren't control freaks, our kids would never potty train."

168

"It's more than that," ABC says. "Did you ever think that maybe, if all of us planned something as a group, it might be even better? That you're not the only one who can problem solve? Seriously, if you are as great as you sometimes think you are, Jacardia wouldn't be the fucking PTA vice president. Did you ever think of that?"

That did it. Now I'm crying and I never cry. I don't believe in tears. I believe in the healing power of carbohydrates. But, looking at my three closest friends, all getting ready to walk out on me, I crumble. Damn this hurts. I need these women. This motherhood thing is scary, uncertain and fraught with peril, real and imagined. These women have been my cheering section. They're always there chanting, "Go Wynn!"

It's not like I have friends to spare. I'm not one of those people who have 739 friends on Facebook, have weekly get-togethers with my college sorority sisters or still keep in touch with my first grade Brownie troop. Of course, I have friends, but most of those friendships are like wearing Spanx. I present a version of my best self by compressing and smoothing out all my undesirable characteristics. I don't have many friends where I feel safe opening up emotionally and letting all the unflattering aspects of my personality relax and hang out.

"Just wait," I plead to ABC, Nikki and Kelly. "All of you, please, sit down and give me a chance to explain."

I hold my breath and finally exhale when they all drop their bags and go back to the couch. I look at Kelly and say, "I am so sorry and you are so right. I should have told you as soon as I discovered the board was submitting fake

169

receipts. You would have unraveled the deception a lot quicker than I did if I had shared the information. I, in no way, wanted to hurt you or any of you. I love all of you."

I stop for a moment because I start getting choked up again. Through the sobs, I tell all of them, "I'll even admit to being a little bit of control freak, but I've never ever thought any of you are stupid. I just assume most people don't want to spend a better part of their Thursday afternoon dressed in last year's Halloween costume tailing the Majesty Moms. I think we all know my long standing rule of always surrounding myself with brilliant people. Don't I say, 'It's never a good sign if I'm the smartest person in the room?' And Nikki, we are a team, a great team! Please, I don't care about my plans or payback schemes. What I care about is that we're friends. This other stuff is bullshit," I say, gesturing to the poster board, "This, our friendship, this is real. This is what matters."

By now everyone is crying. I'm starting to think we're all having our periods at the same time or something. ABC wipes her eyes and blows her nose on a hospital gown and says, "Everyone bring it in for a hug."

I announce mid hug, "Let's just forget about all this PTA crap. They'll eventually self-destruct, right? It's time to move on."

ABC, Nikki and Kelly break up the hug, look at me and Kelly says, "Oh, hell no. We're not leaving this room until the four of us come up the most masterful, most comprehensive, most diabolical plan that's ever been conceived."

ABC yells, "Oh yeah, those fuckers are going down!"

I get up, walk over to the poster board and start tearing it up. "Why are you doing that?" Nikki asks.

"We won't need this because I know whatever WE come up with will be so much better! Now, who wants pie before we get started?"

Week Five of the School Year

T Minus 37 Hours

It took nine hours and a lot of debating back and forth that night in the nursing home, but I think we came up with a cunning and clever plan. To be honest, the best parts (if not most) of the plan are from my original Four Prong Plank of Payback. Kelly was adamant we deal with the stealing of PTA funds "in house." I wanted to go public, but she explained that since she's the treasurer it could make her look bad or worse she could be held responsible. The only thing I'm worried about is that ABC and Kelly insisted we needed more than the four of us and my son to pull the plan off. They emphasized I should be in the background during the payback. Can I tell you how much this hurt my feelings? Me, in the background? I finally relented when they explained my presence in all four "areas of focus" could trigger suspicion in Jacardia, Muchy, Caroline and Liz. I could argue those four aren't smart enough to make the mental leap, but begrudgingly, went along with their theory.

This means we have to use fresh recruits. Blame it on me having trust issues, but using untested moms out in the field makes me nervous. Helping us out are Heather, which is okay I know she's got what it takes, but we're also using Croc Mom. I asked ABC if she thought Croc Mom has what it takes to pull something like this off.

"I think so. She's got brains galore. Did you know she's a chemist? And she's taken so much shit from those four women over the years, I think that the least we can do is give her the opportunity to shovel some crap right back at them. Add in that everyone thinks she's harmless and will never suspect of her doing anything sneaky and you've got yourself a winner."

I agree with ABC, Croc Mom has endured her share of mean mom antics which I think all stem from the likes of Jarcardia, Caroline, Murchy and Liz being intimidated and jealous of her brilliant kids.

The final member of our team is - brace yourself - Jasper. I'm totes sers about this. He's an integral part of our plan and bringing him into the fold was even ABC's idea. She had a "what the hell" attitude about it. I believe her exact words were "We're doing whatever it takes to get this done."

In assembling our team we met with Heather, Croc Mom and Jasper separately and shared a condensed version of what we had discovered. Once each of them had shown the proper amount of outrage, scorn and a desire to seek revenge, we invited them to join us on our quest. This mission isn't just about what's happened in the last six weeks. This is payback for a backlog of predatory practices.

Today we're meeting at Kelly's house. Everyone calls it "Mini Mount Vernon." Her home was built by an American history professor and is a quarter scale replica of our First President's abode. When Kelly and her husband bought it, they had to do an almost total gut job on the inside. The previous owner had been a little too true to history. The interior was authentic colonial - as in no dishwasher, no showers, and no overhead lights. Eight years later, they're still working on it, but everything they've done is beautiful and comfortable. Not an easy combo to pull off - plus there's not a butter-churn in site.

We're all in Kelly's dining room getting ready to do a schedule run through. In a show of good faith, because they love me (and a tiny part of me hopes because they feel excruciatingly guilty for what happened at the nursing home and have seen the error of their ways), my friends have put me in charge. It's imperative that no one makes any mistakes on Saturday. Due to the wide-ranging scope and sensitive nature of this mission, I have abandoned my old-school use of handouts and poster board for an impressive Powerpoint.

Kelly starts the meeting by reminding everyone of their vow of silence. "If a word of this gets out, we're all going down," she says in what I call her IRS auditor voice and then quickly adds, "if you don't think you can handle being a part of this, leave now because once Wynn starts her Powerpoint, that's it, you're in up to your eyebrows."

Heather laughs and says, "God, I feel like I'm a made man in some kick-ass-do-gooder mafia. This is awesome!"

Kelly is being a little over the top, but I discovered once I let go of the reins of being the supreme leader of revenge scenarios, my friends perked up and showed a natural aptitude for it. I dim the lights in Kelly's dining room and begin my Powerpoint. I've named our "project" Team Takedown. The revenge plan is a two parter. Phase 1 will take place at the Fall Festival. This is where we plan to bring down Caroline and Liz. Phase 2 takes place that evening at the "Dancing with the Stars" parent fundraiser. Murchy will get her comeuppance and Jacardia, if all goes as planned, will receive a motherlode of justice. Heather and Croc Mom will only take part in Phase 1 - code named Festival Foe-Down. Jasper, Nikki, Kelly, and ABC will be focused on Phase 2 - code named Dirty Dancing. I will be overseeing both Phase 1 and Phase 2. The key to us pulling

174

this off, without doing jail time is the timing. Everyone has to stay on schedule. The good news is since we're all working the Fall Festival, we'll have on headsets, making it easier to communicate. "Remember," I say, "be sure to talk in code when using the headsets so no one but Team Takedown will be able to understand what's going on."

To help with this, I have a Powerpoint page of approved code words. We all go over them as a group and then I do a quick test to ensure everyone knows them. Croc Mom raises her hand and asks me, "What if I get nervous and forget a code word? What do I do then?"

"You'll do fine," I tell her. "If you freeze up use the go to code - 'I need more volunteers that will get one of us running to help you."

Croc Mom smiles and repeats, "I need more volunteers, I need more volunteers. Okay, got it. I'm going be great. I promise. Have I told you how much I appreciate this opportunity? I swear I won't let you down."

ABC says, "No worries. You wouldn't be here if we didn't think you could do the job."

I'm now done going over the logistics of the Festival Foe-Down plan so Heather and Croc Mom are asked to leave. Our master plan is to keep everybody on a need to know basis. ABC, Nikki, Kelly and I thought it would be best if each "team member" is apprised only of their specific duties, less chance for the whole "loose lips sink ships" thing. What we didn't factor in was Croc Mom and Heather now being supremely ticked at being asked to vacate the premises and Jasper who just arrived dressed in all black and wearing a ski cap (WTH?), is equally ticked that he didn't' get to take part in the Phase 1 briefing. What a mess. I go over and conference with ABC, Nikki and Kelly and we make a unanimous decision.

"Here's the deal," I say, "we have no problem with everyone staying and filling Jasper in about what's happening in Phase 1, but by doing this you're committing yourself to more responsibility. That means if we get in trouble - all of us are going down."

Croc Mom says, "About that, I would have thought we'd be more *Mission Impossible*. The whole if you're caught everyone will 'disavow any knowledge of your actions' thing.' Doesn't that sound better? That way only one of us goes down."

Now I'm getting pissed. This is another reason I didn't want to stray from my original tried-and-true team. They know better than to ask idiotic questions. Kelly can see I'm getting angry and quickly says, "Let's vote on it. All in favor of going Mission Impossible style say aye."

I'm the only one who says nay. Then there's Jasper who says, "Totes good to me. It's going to be BBBB."

I roll my eyes at Jasper and say, "Some of you may not know Jasper. He's a facialist at the dermatology day spa that's affiliated with ABC's ex-husband's medical practice. Jasper is here because he's been very helpful in tracking down the phony receipts and he's got a big role to play in phase two of our plan."

ABC pipes in with, "And, he's my former husband's current boyfriend. I know it's weird, but the best thing to do is just go with it."

Jasper smiles really big and blows kisses. While he's doing this Nikki says, "I'm sorry, but I didn't understand what you said when you walked in."

"Oh, yeah, I talk in abbreves, so much faster. What I said was this whole thing sounds totally good to me because it's going to be big, bold, and bitching - beeyotches."

"Jasper," I say trying not to sound like I'm scolding him, "for this little arrangement we've got going on to work, you need to talk in complete words. I know it's going to be a strain, but I have faith in you."

He sighs and says, "Right on mama. I'll do my best. I'm in it to Wynn it." As he's saying Wynn it, he winks at me and then talks about his outfit. "See, I'm already getting my *Mission Impossible* on. I'm dressed like Tom Cruise in the first M.I. movie, that's how into this I am."

Although Jasper is acting like a mid-level idiot, I'm not worried. I spent some quality time with him when he was helping me decipher the spa receipts and he's not a bad guy. He's really kind of smart. I think his biggest issue is he's lonely and immature. This caper could be a character builder for him.

I ask everybody to sit back down and before I can begin Phase 2 of the briefing Jasper stands up and says, "I have an announcement to make."

ABC and I give each other a worried "What the hell now?" looks and before I can ask Jasper to shut up he says, "I think you may all want to know that Jim."

ABC interrupts him with, "That would be my ex-husband."

Jasper, looking a little flustered at being interrupted, continues, "As I was saying, Jim and I have decided to go our separate ways - totes sers."

"He's moved on to someone new, hasn't he?" ABC asks.

"Well, as a matter of fact, I believe he is now keeping company with his receptionist Berlin and for those of you who like math, she's three years younger than me."

Heather says, "Wait, I'm confused. Jim was married to ABC, left her, hooked up with some old bald dude, then you, and now is back dating women! What's up with that?"

ABC says, "I don't know, but I'm really glad it's no longer any of my business or my problem."

Jasper adds, "Jim's a flip-flopper and he's more floppy than flippy, if you know what I mean."

Everyone looks at ABC for confirmation of the floppy remark. She smiles and says, "Yeah, Jim can be a little floppy."

"He's little, that's for sure," says Jasper, making everyone laugh.

I try to take back control of the briefing, but before I have a chance to redirect everyone's attention to my Powerpoint, Jasper says, "Hey ABC, can I call you ABC? I know your real name is Allison, but everyone here is calling you ABC so I thought maybe I could. I was wondering now that I'm not with Jim anymore could you and I be, well, not friends because that would be weird, but maybe not enemies."

178

"Alright," I say, "It's starting to sound like a Lifetime movie has mated with *VH 1's Couples Therapy*. You two can work this out later. Let's all refocus our energy on Phase 2."

Finally, I'm able to continue with my Powerpoint. Phase 2 is bit trickier than Phase 1. It's much more technical and involves electronics and lighting. This is where my son's expertise comes in. Nikki also plays a starring role in Phase 2. "Are you sure you can do this Nikki? I ask. "It's not late to say no and I promise none of us would be mad."

"Wynn, quit asking me if I can do this. Am I nervous? Yes, but don't waste your time wondering if I can pull this off. I've got this."

I give her a big smile and say, "Okay, just remember we've all got your back."

Nikki laughs and says, "It's not my back I'm worried about. It's my feet."

I go over the Phase 2 checklist one more time and drill everyone on the timeline and the supply list. "Jasper," I ask, "do you have everything you need?"

"Yep, it all came in yesterday. I'm g-t-g. Sors, I mean sorry. I meant to say I'm good to go."

"Alright, I think that's it. As of right now we're going dark - no phone calls, no text, no communication about this whatsoever. This is it. It all starts in T minus thirty-seven hours. The next time we see each other will be at the Fall Festival."

Heather jumps in with, "Remember all Festival committee chairs need to be at the school on Saturday at 8 a.m. to help with set up. The Festival opens at 11."

Kelly says, "And Phase 1 starts two hours after the Festival begins. I can't wait!"

Everyone says goodbye and leaves except for ABC, Nikki, Kelly and I. Looking at me ABC says, "Well, what do you think, Wynn? Can we pull this off?"

I smile and say very confidently, "Of course we can. We're a force of nature. What's more powerful than a bunch of pissed-off moms?"

Kelly adds, "Especially a bunch of really smart, pissed-off moms."

And with that we high-five.

Festival Foe-Down

Caroline

Since all of us on Team Takedown (minus Jasper) are Fall Festival committee chairs we arrive at the school at 8 a.m. It's a gorgeous autumn day. Sunny, with a slight breeze and warm enough so you don't need a sweater, but not so hot you're sweating which means one thing - in about three hours this place will be swarming with moms in shorts and Uggs. The worst outfit for a female since the burka. The entire carnival takes place outside in the back of the school. The inflatable bounce houses, obstacle courses and rock-climbing wall are located up on the soccer field. The carnival games, overseen by ABC, are set up inside a huge red and white stripped circus tent on the baseball diamond. Nikki's face painting booth, which Jasper has graciously volunteered to help with, is by the carnival games. The Farmer's Market food area is set up on the parking lot behind the school so families are greeted with the healthy offerings of fruits and vegetables. My junk food stands are given a low profile location off to the side of the school. You would think I'm pushing crack. I'm not worried. I know once the word gets out I'm dealing deep fried Twinkies it's going to be a freaking mad house. Add in snow cones, churros and cotton candy and you've got major crowd control issues. The good news is I have experienced volunteers manning the junk food booths and the fried Twinkie stand came with its own staff due to the liability issue of working with large vats of 450-degree oil.

181

All the volunteers are dressed in bright green T-shirts with navy blue letters that say, "Fall Festival Friend" and we each have on an apron with pockets. Everyone heading up a station is wearing a headset. Right before the Festival starts I do a test of the headset using some Team Takedown code words. It works perfectly. All the team members report in promptly. I'm now cautiously optimistic we can pull this off. In a surprise to no one, the PTA board of Liz, Jacardia, Caroline and Murchy show up at exactly when the carnival starts at eleven o'clock. God forbid, they break an acrylic nail or risk having enlarged pores by doing some of the grunt work. (I know I'm a sweaty mess from moving booths around and unloading cartons of Flossine - the sugar used in the cotton candy machine.)

All four of them are wearing light grey, tight to the point of circulation inhibiting Nike T-shirts with, of course, a deep V neck. The T-shirt has the word, "Awesomeness" printed on it in bright yellow. Each woman also has on some version of an Ugg glitter boot. Jacardia is wearing cut off Daisy Duke shorts that highlight her lower booty cleavage. Caroline, of course, has on short, thong friendly, black yoga pants with her hair hanging down to her butt crack. Murchy is also wearing some Daisy Dukes, but her cut offs are blinged out with crosses, one on each ass check. Liz, I guess, in an attempt at demonstrating the art of full butt coverage, is wearing white, Burberry cropped jeans with her hair in a plaid Burberry headband. They're prowling the carnival grounds like just crowned prom queens seeking adulations from the crowd. As I'm spinning cotton candy I see Heather handing them headsets. They giggle and put them on. Over my headset I hear each of them going, "test, testing 1, 2, 3." Then I hear ABC saying, "I'm glad the rest of our PTA board could finally show up. Kelly's been here for three hours already."

Jacardia answers back with, "I have to be careful and not overdo it. Since, I'm the STAR in Dancing with the Stars this evening."

ABC laughs and says, "We'll see about that."

"What does that mean?" Jacardia snaps back.

"It means nothing. Heather says over her headset, "ABC how are you on supplies?" This is Team Takedown code for shut up.

Almost two hours later, I'm covered in cotton candy sugar and I've already had to break up two scuffles in the deep fried Twinkie line. I'm not surprised because these Twinkies are worth fighting over. I thought the Twinkie would just be dunked in the oil, but no, it's submerged in funnel cake batter, then gets a bath in the deep fryer and for an extra sweet rush it's coated in confectionary sugar. Wars have been fought for less.

Croc Mom, in accordance with the time line, has come over to ostensibly help me twirl cotton candy. Our real focus is Caroline. We knew the only way to lure a woman who orders a hot water and lemon at Starbucks over to the junk food station would be to go straight for her Achilles heel - pawning her kids off on someone. Croc Mom gets on her headset and says, "Caroline, you need to come to the cotton candy booth. There's a mom here and she wants to talk to you about your kids spending the night at her house. She says she's not going to be here that long, so I would hurry."

Croc Mom smiles at me and asks, "How long do you think it will take for her to get here?"

"I'd give it less than five minutes. Are you ready?"

"I've been ready since my daughter was in first grade and Caroline told her it was a good thing she was so smart because she sure wasn't pretty or skinny."

Croc Mom has me worried. She's looks weird. Her body has gone rigid and she's got a bad case of crazy eyes. I pat her on the back and say, "It will be okay just follow my lead. Here's she comes now."

Caroline cautiously walks into the junk food booth area like she's entering a containment facility for both the Ebola virus and assorted hemorrhagic fevers at the Center for Disease Control. She's holding a hand over her nose and mouth. I yell out to her, "Calories aren't airborne. It's a proven medical fact you don't gain weight by being near food. You have to ingest it."

She sneers at me and asks Croc Mom, "Where's the mother who wants my kids to spend the night at her house?"

Croc Mom, still working that scary face, says, "Come inside the booth. She had to go over to the game tent, but she left me her number."

Caroline goes, "Ewww no. It's full of sugar in there. Just text me."

"I don't have my phone. If you want the number then come inside the booth."

You can see Caroline weighing the pros and cons in her head. She really wants to dump her kids off for the rest of the day, but does she want it bad enough to walk inside the cotton candy booth. Croc Mom looks nervous. I'm not. I'm confident Caroline will choose being subjected to a sugar cloud over spending an weekend with her children. To give her a verbal push inside the booth I do

184

my version of Obi-Wan Kenobi's "These aren't the droids you're looking for" and say, "You have the most beautiful skin. It's absolutely poreless. Can you please come in so I can take a closer look?"

Caroline slowly walks into the booth. Croc Mom asks Caroline to come closer so she can continue to whirl cotton candy on the cardboard funnel with one hand as she takes out the mom's phone number from her apron with another. Caroline scoots closer. I quit selling cotton candy and grab a ten pound carton of Flossine. Our plan is for me to trip and accidently pour the Flossine all over Caroline and then apologize by trying to clean her up with "special" wet wipes. This will turn her into a sticky, gooey, mess. Bonus, the Flossine will cause her hair to briefly harden, but something is wrong. Croc Mom is way off script! She's asking Caroline to hold the cotton candy stick for her so she can look for the number. This is not how we rehearsed it. Caroline grabs the stick and snaps at Croc Mom to "hurry the hell up."

Croc Mom tells Caroline she has to lean over the machine more to twirl the cotton candy the right way. As Caroline is leaning in Croc Mom grabs three feet of Caroline's artificially colored (I'm thinking John Frieda luminous blue black hair dye from Target.) flat ironed, Brazilian blown-out hair, which I'm pretty sure is one-third extensions, and sticks it inside the industrial grade cotton candy machine where it's getting twisted around the motor that spins the sugar. Oh shit, shit, shit, Caroline is now attached to the cotton candy motor via her hair. Each rotation of the motor pulls her head closer to the inside machines. She's screaming, "Turn this fucker off!"

I run over to unplug the machine, but before I have to chance to yank the plug Croc Mom shouts, "Calm down, calm down. I'll get you out!" I see her take large pinking shears out of her apron pocket. She reaches in and starts cutting Caroline's hair off at about her ear! At first Caroline doesn't realize she's now got hair that looks like Moe from the *Three Stooges* because she's too busy swearing. I start backing out of the booth because I don't want to be near Caroline when she figures it out. I thought Croc Mom would follow me, but she's standing right in Caroline's face and says, "Sorry about the hair."

Caroline reaches up and starts patting her head and then screeches so loud people eating fried Twinkies stop in mid bite. After she's done screaming the death threats begin. Croc Mom says very matter-of-factly, "Calm down, it's not the end of the world, but too bad for you - you were never smart and now you're sure not pretty." She then hands me her pinking shears and walks out of the booth.

Wow, still waters run deep! I wonder how long she's been tamping down that anger. I just stand there, pinking shears in hand, processing what I witnessed. Caroline's shrieks force me back to reality. She's now threatening to sue Croc Mom. Before I have a chance to broadcast the Team Takedown distress code of, "I need more volunteers." I see ABC and Heather running towards the cotton candy booth. They both take one look at Caroline and give me the WTF face. Before I can explain what went down I hear a very familiar male voice. It's my husband and he's telling Caroline how her legal case against Croc Mom is weak. "It won't ever make it to court Caroline. I saw the whole thing and the mom with the scissors saved your life. She's a hero."

Another guy shouts, "Yeah, a couple more seconds in that cotton candy maker and you might have choked to death. Your hair was wrapping around your neck."

186

This sets Caroline off again. I go over and tell her she's got the bone structure to pull off shorter hair and gently suggest that maybe the best thing to do is leave the carnival and go straight to her hair stylist or at least a Super Cuts at the mall. Thank God, she takes my advice and bolts for her car. With her new haircut and her bony frame she looks like an malnourished 12-year-old boy vampire who just got bitch slapped by a werewolf.

My husband takes a bite of the deep fried Twinkie he's been holding and says, "What the hell happened?"

"Yeah," says ABC, "how did Caroline get the extreme makeover Edward Scissors Hand edition?

"I don't really know. She was leaning over the cotton candy machine and the next thing you know her hair is trapped in the motor. Good thing Croc Mom just happened to have scissors, of this magnitude, in her apron pocket." I say, while holding up the extra-large pinking shears. It's my way of telling ABC and Heather that Croc Mom has gone rogue.

"Where is she now?" asks Heather.

"I'm not sure. I think the ordeal of cutting Caroline's hair off at the ear has her pretty shaken up. She gave me these," I say holding up the scissors, "and took off."

My son Clay walks over with his sister and says, "Does all this mean the cotton candy booth is closed?"

"Hey, that's not fair. I haven't had any yet." Grace complains.

Clay follows up with, "It smells gross over here."

"Getting three feet of hair caught in the motor of a cotton candy machine isn't exactly going to smell like Apple Cinnamon Febreze kids and yes, I'm closing down the booth. I think with the Twinkie, churro and snow cone stations going strong there will still be enough junk food for everyone."

Finally, my children and husband take off and I'm able to do a debrief with Heather and ABC. I go into detail about how Croc Mom deviated from my spectacular plan and went Old Testament on Caroline.

"It was a reverse Samson and Delilah! Croc Mom's rage was biblical in its intensity. This is what happens when we use rookie recruits in the field. It's obvious Croc Mom should have had a psych eval before we welcomed her aboard Team Takedown. This is not what we're about. We don't put moms, no matter how much we don't like them, in harm's way and attack them with scissors. I'm worried about Croc Mom. We need to find her and make sure she's okay. At the very least she needs a Xanex with a boxed wine chaser and I'm not ruling out some inpatient psychiatric care."

ABC says, "I'll get Kelly on situation Croc Mom,"You, Heather and Nikki have about ten minutes until the Queen takes a fall."

I take my cell phone out of an apron pocket, check the time and say, "You're right. Let's get going. I need to check on the rest of my food booths and then I'll assume my lookout position. Heather you go get Nikki and from this moment forward I'm going to be checking everyone for crazy eyes. If your pupils aren't evenly dilated you're out."

Liz

All my booths are running smoothly. I got a dad volunteer to act as security at the Twinkie stand and it's stopped the cutting in line and threats of fisticuffs. I hate to confess this, but I'm worried. Croc Mom's scissors episode has me a little ruffled. It's a good thing I'm just back up for Phase 1, Part 2 - code named, "The Queen of Mean." This is a delicate operation. It required massive behind-the-scenes work to set it up. I take a deep breath, chug a mini can of Diet Coke I had stashed in my apron pocket, get on my headset, and say, "It's time for the royal treatment."

It takes only seconds after I uttered those code words for Heather to get on the schools public address system and announce that a special ceremony will be taking place in five minutes on the stage by the game tent. She urges all families and friends of Spring Creek Elementary to attend. I see people starting to walk over to the stage. When I spot the Channel 37 Action News You Can Use van pulling up I smile so big I think my face might explode. All the players are here. How excellent.

I scurry over to intercept the former morning traffic girl now wanna be investigative reporter Kat Alex. Kat, as I predicted, has played right into my hands. Someone, not me, contacted her with a news tip using a burner cell phone. The tip was a little something about an elementary school PTA president running an escort service called "The Majesty Club." I knew Kat would see this tidbit as something that could skyrocketed her career. I also knew, thanks to friends I still keep up in the news business, that she is lazy and her idea of researching a story is to Google it. So, I made it very easy for her to Google Majesty Club and find a phony website offering up "dating" opportunities. Did I put Liz's name anywhere on the site? Of course not, but I left a trail of bed crumbs that might, if you were an idiot of a reporter, lead you to believe that Spring Creek's Liz Derby could possibly be a madame. Being very careful not to leave behind any digital evidence that would link me as the creator of the website I uploaded it from a computer at the school. I even created a blog on Wordpress called *Majesty Club - Tips from a Modern Madame & PTA President*. It's full of call girl and PTA etiquette and yes I had a blast writing it.

My favorite tip is #32: "Never wear a lip plumping lipstick while heading south. The cayenne pepper in it could singe your date and lead to an unfortunate shrinkage episode resulting in a loss of gratuity income and as any good Madame and PTA president knows you never want to take the fun out of FUNdraising."

There was a big "What If" in my "Queen of Mean" plan. I knew I had probably reeled in Kat, but when dealing with news reporters you can never be sure if they're going to show up. If there had been breaking news, like a twenty car pileup on the interstate, we would have been forced to go to our "Queen of Mean" backup plan. While it's also brilliant, it wouldn't offer the public shaming spectacle I was going for.

This is why I'm excitedly jumping up and down and yelling, "Kat, Kat! Welcome, to our Fall Festival and thanks for coming. It must be a slow news day for you to be covering an elementary school Festival."

"The story I'm after has nothing to do with this Festival. Now where's the PTA president ceremony taking place?"

Right over there," I say, pointing to the stage. She thanks me and trudges off. Her cameraman marches ahead of her. I get back on the headset and say, "Kat's in the cradle. I repeat Kat is in the cradle."

The next thing I hear is Heather, once again, on the school's P.A. system, announcing, "A very special ceremony is taking place in one minute. That's one minute folks; right here on the festival stage. We'll also be announcing our raffle winners for the trip for four to Disney World, so please everyone come to the festival stage area."

Heather is on the stage with a hand held microphone and I see Nikki escorting Liz up the stage steps. I turn around to check on the TV crew and they seem to be set up. I get on my headset and say, "It's a go."

Heather smiles and begins talking, "Welcome Spring Creek family and friends. Is this a great Fall Festival or what?!!!! (Everyone cheers.) And what about those fried Twinkies? (More cheers.) Now, before I announce the raffle winner I'd like to do one very important thing. As most of you know every year, at this time, we honor the Spring Creek Elementary PTA president for all the hard work she does on behalf of the students, parents and teachers."

Heather hands the microphone to Nikki. "Our PTA president this year is Liz Derby and she's an amazing dynamo. The saying at Spring Creek is, "If you want to get things done right, just ask Liz." In fact, she's even started something called the Majesty Club this year, isn't that right Liz?"

Liz leans over and snatches the microphone, "Yes, the Majesty Club is a brand new labor of love for me and I can't tell you how much satisfaction I'm getting from it. It's especially thrilling working with young girls. You know little girls

191

can do a lot of stuff that we usually only associate with adults doing. The Majesty Club is all about giving girls the opportunity to discover a brand new world."

I hear ABC say, "Oh shit!" over the headset and Kat looks at her cameraman and asks, "Are you fucking getting this?"

Nikki gently tugs the microphone away from Liz and says, "Now, I understand the Majesty Club is invitation only?"

"Yes," Liz says, pulling the mic away from Nikki, "but I'm always looking for new members. Don't be shy moms if you really think this is something you or your daughter might want to do just contact me. Of course, due to the nature of this volunteer activity, we're highly selective and there is a rigorous screening process."

Heather, holding a plaque, walks over to where Liz and Nikki are standing on the stage. Right before she reaches out to hand Liz the plaque, she stops, and says, "I see Kat Alex here from Channel 37 news. Kat do you have any questions for our PTA President?"

Kat looks at her cameraman and says, "Are you ready?

"Yeah, yeah," I'm rolling. Go."

Kat, carrying a wireless microphone, storms up on stage, as well as you can in four-inch heels and says, "Liz Derby isn't it true the Majesty Club is really an escort service? That you're not only a PTA president, but a Madame? And based upon what I'm heard you say only minutes ago are you now engaging in a child prostitution ring? What do you have to say for yourself?

Liz goes into full stuck up witch mode. Instead of immediately refuting what Kat has said, which would be the logical move, she instead insults her.

"Aren't you the traffic girl? Do you even know what you're talking about? I don't know if you're crazy or just really, really stupid. I'm going to say both. The Majesty Club is all about girls. We're doing public service, lots of public service. Can you spell that or didn't they teach you those kind of things at, I don't know, the night school you went to get your little "I'm a traffic reporter" certificate?"

Kat, not backing down, turns to the audience and says, "I'll have a full report on Liz Derby and her secret life of so called "Public Service" tonight at six."

"You, you, bitch!" Liz screams and lunges at Kat. Kat hits her on the head with the microphone and rips off Liz's plaid Burberry headband throwing it into the crowd like an errant bridal bouquet. Liz tries to karate kick Kat with her Ugg silver short sparkle boot and misses. Kat runs away, but Liz catches her by the hair and screams, "Take it back. Take it all back."

"It's the news! You don't take back the news!" Kat yells at her.

Heather and Nikki try to pull Liz off of Kat. Luckily, a police officer, who was working the McGruff the Crime Dog safety booth, has jumped on the stage and successfully separates the two women. Each one is threatening lawsuits (Why does it always immediately go straight to lawsuits?) featuring liable, slander and assault and battery. The officer calls for backup. As he's leading each woman off the stage Liz starts kicking him. He lets go of Kat, uses one hand to grab both of Liz's wrists and the other to handcuff her. Holy crap, Liz is being perp walked through the carnival!

My expectations for Plan 1, Part 2 have just been gargantuanly exceeded. I'm so happy I'm afraid I might lose bladder control and pee my track pants. (Note to self: do more kegels.) I was going for some embarrassing Majesty Club backlash where Liz would be asked about running an escort service and she would go all righteous indignation and deny it. The crowd watching would start circulating their version of the story and like the game of telephone it would go from, "Did you hear a TV reporter asked Liz Derby if she ran an escort service? To "Did you hear Liz Derby runs an escort service? Never, did I dare to dream, that Liz would attack a reporter and then repeatedly kick a cop. I get on my headset and triumphantly announce, "Phase 1 is done" and then look up and see my husband staring at me.

"Are you stalking me, Sam?" I ask.

"I think the bigger question is what the hell are you up to? The scissors episode, so not your style. You're not one to cut and run, plus, it had no finesse. This, he says gesturing towards the stage, is so you. The news crew showing up. The attention to detail. The timing. What I haven't figured out yet is how you planted the story about the Majesty Club being an escort service."

This is not what I need right now - a curious husband. I have to shake him loose.

"You know what Columbo, right now I don't have time to continue this charming little chit chat thing we've got going on. What I need is for you to

194

make sure Clay makes it to the country club by five. He's helping set up the sound system for Dancing with the Stars."

"That's the best you've got? The brush off with an errand tacked on the end. Nice try, but it's not going to work. I'm keeping my eyes on you and Wynn be careful. You know our family's Golden Rule?"

"Yes, yes, yes," I say exasperated, "Thou shall not get sued, arrested or commit any act that threatens our ability to stay gainfully employed and/or jeopardizes the 401 K or Roth IRA."

He leans over and kisses my cheek and says, "You taste good."

"I'm sure it's the cotton candy sugar and residual Twinkie batter, but thanks."

He sighs, pulls away from me and says, "I'm not kidding about you being careful. You know you're not really a super hero? Sometimes I think you may need to be on medication."

I smile, lean in and whisper, 'There's no medication for making someone un-awesome."

He laughs, gives me another kiss, gathers up the kids and walks away, but not before looking over his shoulder and yelling. "The rule Wynn, don't forget the rule."

I don't have the time for the rule right now. It's two down, two to go and I've got a schedule to keep.

Dirty Dancing

Murchy

After the most profitable (Thank you deep fried Twinkie booth.) Fall Festival in the history of Spring Creek Elementary closes at 4 p.m., I find the remaining members of Team Takedown. (Croc Mom is still missing in action.) All of us need to head to the country club and do our Dancing with the Stars prep work. There's stage lighting to double and triple check and a lot of audio finagling that still needs to be done. We have a very small window when we can accomplish all this and not be seen by the Dancing with the Stars "stars" and by this I mean moms, most of them with their 35th birthday in the rearview mirror, channeling their inner stripper and the stage crew, also mothers, who are trying to work their way up the hot mom ladder by volunteering backstage and kissing Brazilian butt lifted ass.

In my original plan only Kelly, ABC, Nikki, Jasper and I would be involved with Phase 2, but Heather is flying high after seeing Liz's reign come-to-an-end and doesn't want to be left out of any of the excitement at the country club. We do a team huddle and I run through our to do list.

"Okay," I say, "I know all of us are still giddy from seeing Liz Derby in handcuffs, but now is not the time to get cocky. We need to stay focused on Phase 2 - Dirty Dancing. First off, no one has time to go home and change, so don't even think about it. I've got some Gain Febreze in my car if anybody needs some smell good love. Secondly, Heather since you want to stay involved I need you to help my son. Make sure he's got everything he needs and if any adult starts asking questions about why a kid is messing with the sound

196

equipment take care of it. Jasper, four words for you, "Don't-Let-Me-Down". I need you to let your associate degree in anatomy soar. Kelly and ABC you know what to do. And Nikki, a lot of this is all about you. Go out there and be amazing. That's all I've got. Let's synchronize our cell phones. It's now 4:16. We've got less than two hours to get set up. Let's do this!"

Because most of us have coached way too many kids' soccer and basketball games we all feel the need to put our hands in the middle of the circle and shout, "Go Team Takedown!"

I walk into the country club ballroom and it's the calm before the storm. A stage has been set up for the dancing and lights have been rigged, including spotlights. Off to the left hand side is the club's audio equipment on a large cart. My son is plugging in cords and doing a sound check with his laptop. Jasper is changing the bulb in one of the spotlights while trying to dodge the wait staff setting up the tables. The Dancing with the Stars Parent Fundraising begins at 7 p.m. with an open bar featuring an "event martini," named "Silver Balls" and heavy hors d'oeuvres. The talent show begins at 8. This is when the moms take the stage and perform their dance routines. Some of them are choreographed by professionals and some moms DIY it. My daughter's ballet teacher, Smith, worked with a group of moms last year. He said it was brutal, claiming it would have been "less stressful teaching hungry Sumatran tigers to tap dance." At the end of all the performances the crowd shows their "appreciation" for the most talented dancer by bidding. The dancer with the highest bid wins the mirror ball trophy. Usually it's a couple of drunk husbands bidding against each other. It's not pretty, but it does raise money for the school.

We know all the mom dancers and stage crew will arrive backstage at 6 p.m. to get into their costumes and finish their hair and makeup. This means I need to get my son out of here soon. Seeing him at an adults only function might make Jacardia suspicious. Clay runs through the music one more time, tells me it's perfect and then hands me his laptop.

"Are you sure?" I ask. "There is no way anything will mess up?"

"No, Mom. I've rigged the sound system to be run through my laptop. Whoever they've hired to run the audio, and I'm thinking it's not some tech genius, but probably a dude who works here, will think he's running the sound board, but actually you'll be doing it. I've created a ghost system."

Clay makes me rehearse running the soundboard on his computer until I get a headache. When he's sure I've got it, I get Heather to give him a ride home and tell her to hurry back. After that I go back to the ballroom and brief Kelly. I remind her to keep up our volunteer cover story. I don't want anyone asking why we're backstage. Jasper has a legitimate reason to be here. Murchy hired him to do her makeup. ABC and Nikki, for now, will need to stay camped out in the women's golf locker room. All of us have on our headsets from the carnival. I look at my cell phone it's 5:57. I get on the headset and ask everybody to report in and then tell Jasper, "You're up."

By 6:30 the backstage, which is really a small ballroom at the club, is a mad house. Mothers in feathers, sequins, rhinestones and what smells like way to much Justin Bieber perfume (or maybe the odor is eau de Jarcardi) are rushing around doing their hair, gluing on false eyelashes and talking about Liz Derby's arrest and Caroline's unfortunate haircut. Jasper has Murchy standing up in a corner of the room and he's literally painting her body. Murchy is wearing a flesh-toned bikini. Her goal, she told Jasper two weeks ago, is to trick the audience into thinking she's nude and covered only in body paint. The example she gave him was a YouTube video link of models at the Playboy mansion looking like Crayola Crayons with gianormous boobs. Murchy wants a huge, hot pink, ornate vertical strip painted on her front and back and a horizontal strip on her arms so she looks like a cross while dancing to the Christian rock version of the song "Knocking On Heaven's Door". Jasper has to coat Murchy's body with body paint infused with glitter, then draw on the pink cross. The final touch is gluing on crystals because Murchy, in an attempt at humor, says, "It don't mean a thing if you ain't got that bling."

Right now, she's questioning Jasper why it's taking so long for him to draw and paint in the cross. She's also asks him why he's painting on parts of her body where there is no cross? He patiently explains he's contouring her body with paint to make it look even more spectacular.

"But the paint you're using I can't see? Murchy whines. "I see the hot pink paint, but that stuff you're using right now it's not showing up?"

"That's because, as I just told you, it's contour paint." Jasper says in a soothing voice. "When you contour your face with make-up do you see it or does it just blend it to make you look incredibly gorg gorg? I'm doing the con blend baby. When I get done with you everyone will think you're a cross with a sers six pack of fab abs."

"Oh, alright then," she pouts, "but hurry up. I don't want to be the last one ready to go."

Heather and I are keeping busy securing Silver Balls cocktails for the dancing moms and other stage crew volunteers. Jacardia has been too engrossed in her primping to take notice of us. She arrived with what she calls her glam squad. It includes a manicurist, make-up artist, hair stylist, masseuse and her personal choreographer from Los Angeles.

At 7:55 the ballroom lights dim and the principal, as M.C. for the event, asks everyone to please take a seat. Dancing with the Stars is front-loaded with the less desirable moms performing first. By this, I mean, the hot mom wannabes like Katie Kirkpartick, who opens the show, festooned in feathers, doing a tap dance, (yes, tap) to the Katy Perry song "Peacock". The primary lyrics being "Wanna see your peacock, cock, cock. Your peacock."

Next up is a very pregnant mom, ballroom dancing with her husband to the Paul Anka song, "Having My Baby." When the lyrics hit the verse, "Oh the seed inside you, Baby do you feel it growing?" the husband breaks into a hip-hop solo where it seems his only move is grabbing his crotch a la Michael Jackson. Classy.

Jacardia as the chair, founder, and four-time winner of the Dancing with the Stars fundraiser always dances the finale. Murchy, after much finagling and sucking up to Jacardia has secured herself the coveted position of being finale adjacent. She's dancing just before Jacardia. After fourteen numbers, Murchy is up. Jasper sprays her with one more shot of glitter, fluffs her hair, and runs to the board that controls the lights. Murchy walks out onto a pitch dark stage and waits for her music to start. As soon as the first knock in "Knocking on Heaven's Door" begins a center spotlight hits Murchy. You hear the crowd gasp. Murchy, I'm sure thinks it's because she looks like a dancing cross. But, she's wrong. The crowd is gasping and now laughing because Jasper covered Murchy in special effects body paint that glows when it's hit with a spot light. Jasper using his artistic talent, excellent penmanship and junior college degree in anatomy and physiology has outlined and labeled every place on Murchy's body where's she's had work done. She looks like a glow-in-the-dark dancing plastic surgery road map. Murchy is oblivious to her enhanced costume until she gets off stage and Jacardia screams, "Did you know you looked like an autopsy report out there?"

Murchy tilts her head to the side, adjusts her bikini top and says, "What are you talking about? I just crushed it. The crowd loved me. What's wrong, are you worried I might beat you this year?

Jacardia grabs a flashlight from a stagehand shines it on Murchy's boobs and says, "This is what the crowd was loving, not your dancing."

Murchy looks down and sees the words breast enhancement and aureola enlargement and lift written on her chest. She rips the flashlight from Jacardia's hand and continues shining it on her body seeing the words tummy tuck part 1 and tummy tuck part 2, even belly button redo printed above her navel. It takes about forty-seconds before she starts screaming Jasper's name. I tell her, "You just missed him. He left about a minute ago."

Upon hearing that she sinks to her knees and begins sobbing. Kelly tells her, "Chill out. It's not that big of a deal. We all know you're made of silicone."

In my on-going attempt to compile a first rate zombie fighting team I add, "Yeah, if there's ever a Zombie apocalypse I want you on my side. You'd be golden because with all that crap in you the zombies wouldn't find you edible. It would be like eating a tire."

Jacardia is getting antsy because her music hasn't started up yet. I sneak over to a dark corner by the lighting board, open up the laptop and cue up the next song. I see Kelly talking to her. She's telling Jacardia there's a problem with the music and to give it a couple of minutes. As soon as Kelly has Jacardia placated I touch "play" on the simulated computer soundboard and classical music soars through the ballroom. A spotlight comes on stage and everyone rushes to the wings to look out and see what's going on. There is Nikki, in a beautiful, white flowing gown, with pointe shoes on dancing to Tchaikovsky's *Romeo and Juliet*. She's amazing. I knew she had studied dance, but to watch her perform is breathtaking. I'm so proud of Nikki I think I might cry. ABC, who had been keeping Nikki under-wraps in the locker room, puts her hand on my shoulder and says, "I feel almost like a proud parent."

"Me too," I say, "God just look at her. She's beautiful."

Our feel good moment abruptly ends when Jacardia demands the stage lights be turned off because Nikki isn't a part of Dancing with the Stars. I tell her to shove it and move closer to the light board. She'll have to go through me to get to it and I'm a girl who eats deep fried Twinkies, so there's not a chance in hell she'll make it past me. "Shut up Jacardia," I say, "Nikki's the only classy thing that's been on that stage all evening. Also, unlike the rest of you, she has a little something called talent."

As Jacardia and I are fighting, Nikki finishes her dance and gets a standing ovation. She has to go back on stage twice for more bows. Heather acts as

Nikki's security guard keeping her away from Jacardia. Although Jacardia did manage to shout, "Enjoy that applause because it's all you'll be getting. You, in no way, are eligible for the mirror ball trophy!"

I step on Jacardia's toes, run over to Nikki, hug her and say, "I never knew you could dance like that! You made me cry."

Nikki laughs and says, "I had a dance scholarship to NYU, but got pregnant."

"Do you ever think of going back to school for dance?"

"I want to go back to school, but not for dance, and don't look sad for me that I couldn't pursue my dance dreams. Dancing professionally has an expiration date, but being a mom is forever. Everything in my life is just the way it should be."

"God, Nikki, now you're going make me cry again."

"Save those tears, Wynn, we still have to work to do."

"Your right about that," I say and whisper into my headset the code word "finale."

Jacardia

You can tell Jacardia is shaken by Nikki's dancing. Her choreographer is giving her a pep talk while the massage therapist rubs her shoulders. One of the stage crew mom's walks over and tells her to get ready to go on. The principal is cued to begin Jacardia's introduction.

"Now the moment you've been waiting for. The grand finale featuring the founder and four-time winner of Spring Creek Elementary School's Dancing with the Stars. The one, the only, the incomparable, the beautiful, Jarcardi Monroe!"

Jacardia struts out on stage. She's basically wearing a miniature glitter bikini covered in what looks like thousands of tiny Swarovski crystals. Her hair is loose, heavily sprayed and has little rhinestones woven into her white mane. She looks like a stripper whose pole name is Shimmer. Jacardia's music begins and it's a rap song. Her first move on stage features her signature dance statement, the center split. Disgusting dads in the audience start hooting, "Yeah baby, that's more like it."

About thirty more seconds of Jacardia's pelvic gyrations go by with a couple of alleged dance moves thrown in when the music changes. At first it's hard to tell the song has changed. It's still rap, but in this song you recognize the voice. It's Jacardia and she's rapping a love song to the principal. I took the recording of her with the principal, added in phrases and words from my *Closet Confidential* interview and wrote her a new song. It features scintillating lyrics from the Roomba recording such as, "Oh, I can tell you would really, really, like that" and "Sweetums, don't worry. I've got that big, strong back of yours." I overlaid that with audio from Jacardia in her closet repeating over and over, "It's so big. It's really big. I like it big. I want it bigger." My favorite part of the song is the principal saying, "My password is Jacardia1, Jacardia1, Jacardia1. You have to keep it a secret, a secret, a secret." It's a shame I won't be putting it on i Tunes.

Jacardia notices her music has changed mid-way through her third split, but it takes her a little while to figure out it's her voice. It's not till the song gets to the principal very distinctly saying, "Jacardia!", that both she and Mr. Parrish freak out. The principal runs back up on the stage and hollers into his microphone, "Turn it off, turn it off!"

His request has the opposite effect. The music gets louder and seems to be on continuous loop. The guy running the audio equipment screams back, "I'm trying, but I can't make it stop! Sorry!"

Meanwhile, poor Jacardia has pulled a muscle or something else very tragic, because she can't get up out of her splits. It's as if her crotch is Gorilla glued to the floor. It's painful to watch, especially when she tries to move and her microscopic bikini bottoms get a tad twisted resulting in her flashing the audience with her middle aged junk, which also seems to have crystals on it. You would think her boyfriend or her husband would rush on stage and help her up. And where's that glam squad when we need them? Surely, having your child bearing lady parts exposed is the very definition of a glam emergency. Oh, wow the crowd is getting into my techno rap. How cool is that?

I knew if I projected the lyrics onto the back curtains of the stage people would sing along. The alcohol-impaired especially enjoy belting out, "It's so big. It's really big. I like it big. I want it bigger." Finally, I see a woman walk out to help Jacardia up. Oh my God, Croc Mom is no longer MIA. She's the chick on stage! She grips Jacardia underneath the armpits and yanks her up out of the splits, but she doesn't let go of her. Croc Mom grabs Jacardia's hair and drags her, caveman style, over to where the principal is frozen in place on stage. Jasper, done hiding from Murchy, is back at the light board and he throws

205

a spotlight on the three of them. Croc Mom lets go of Jacardia and punches the principal, hard in the face while shouting, "This is from the kids!"

The audience breaks out in raucous, spontaneous applause. It takes everything I've got to not get on the headset and tell everybody involved in Team Takedown to go on stage and take a well-deserved bow. Instead, I tell the troops to fall back. It's in our best interest to take advantage of all the confusion and disappear. Call it my version of disavowing any knowledge of what's happened in the last eight hours.

Fifteen minutes later we meet up at the large Festival tent at the back of the school that won't be taken down until tomorrow. Everyone highs five and hugs each other. I check Croc Mom's eyes. She still looks crazy. Heather breaks out a bottle of champagne and starts chanting, "Speech, speech, speech."

ABC yells, "Get your ass up here Wynn and say something."

I shout back, "We're a team everybody should say something."

Kelly takes a swig of champagne straight from the bottle, swallows and says, "Come on, you know you were the mastermind. Say something our fearless leader."

I smile as Heather presents me with my own bottle of champagne and bows. "Okay, okay, you know I can't resist an audience." I raise my champagne bottle, laugh and say, "Here's to good friends and new friends" as I look over at Jasper, "But most especially here's to mothers in track pants who can kick some ass! We are fierce. Overlook us and our lack of Botoxed enhanced foreheads at your own peril, for the women that drive carpool without mink eyelash extensions truly rule the world!"

Everyone cheers. We all toast again and again and then split up to return home. I remind everyone to keep their mouths shut, no matter how tempting it's going to be to share their part in Team Takedown.

As I'm walking out of the tent to my car I see my husband in the school parking lot. He's leaning against the hood of his car, his arms crossed over his chest.

"Well, well," he says, "if it isn't the women who brought down the Spring Creek Elementary PTA. Fancy meeting you here."

"I'm guessing that means you attended the Dancing with the Stars fundraiser?"

"Oh, I wouldn't have missed it especially after our son told me you've been working on recording a rap song on his computer. Oh excuse me, that's wrong. It was techno rap. My wife - the techno rapper. No way was I going to not experience that."

"Well then, do share, what did you think of my song?"

"It was perfect, just perfect. You really have talent, you know. Not only in your ability to produce rap songs, but your organizational skill are also quite excellent, especially your knack of using our children's skills to their fullest potential. Grace, I've been told, is now adept at covert reconnaissance and troubleshooting and Clay's handiwork was all over this. Very clever, the program, I'm sure, he wrote, so his laptop would control the soundboard and then there's this."

My husband reaches behind his back and presents me with the Roomba. He must have been hiding it on the hood of his car.

"The Roomba!" I cry. "I forgot about the Roomba! How did you get it out of the principal's office? We could have been totally busted if someone had discovered the Roomba was a mobile surveillance drone. I'm sure Mr. Parrish would have eventually thought to check his office for some sort of recording device. Oh, thank you, thank you, thank you!"

"You're welcome. After Grace, the big mouth, proudly shared her harrowing first person tale of "I was a Third Grade Spy", I talked to the school janitor this afternoon and told him I needed to retrieve my son's science fair project from the principal's office. He let me right in and Clay rescued the Roomba. You know what you did might be construed as morally unsound or just plain wrong?"

"Maybe."

"And I'm sure you'll tell me that if it was wrong it was for all the right reasons."

"Of course. Isn't that one of the reasons you married me - my ability to rationalize?"

"Well, that and a couple of others. Come on. Let's go home. The kids are waiting up to see if good triumphed over evil.

"Did it? Do you think that good triumphed over evil?"

"I think," Sam says, wrapping his arm around my waist, "that my wife is such a bad ass I'm now very scared to ever tick her off."

"That's good, because I like my men scared of me."

"Men? Don't you mean man and maybe the leaf blower?"

I laugh and give him a hug.

Epilogue

The Dancing with the Stars event set a fundraising record, although no one was awarded the mirror ball trophy. An enterprising dad suggested that instead of bidding on the best dancer the crowd should "go karaoke" with people paying for the chance to get on stage and have a turn singing what now and forever more will be known as "Jacardia's song".

Liz for assaulting a police officer, got off with community service. She can be seen picking up trash, in an orange jumpsuit with Burberry headband, along the interstate on Monday and Thursday morning from eight till eleven for the next six months. Her Majesty Club is permanently kaput. The video of her fighting with Action News reporter Kat Alex made the six and 11 o'clock news and went viral on YouTube. To date it has had over 800,000 views.

*Murch*y continues to deny she's ever had any plastic surgery and blames the whole episode on people "jealous of her beauty," citing Proverbs 14:30 "A tranquil heart gives life to the flesh, but envy makes the bones rot." She's threatened to sue Jasper, but he claims he was exercising his right to artistic expression. Unfortunately for Murchy, she has bigger problems than trying to convince people she's not 98% plastic. Due to an anonymous tip (from a burner cell phone) the IRS is investigating Murchy's alleged charity funded by her church jewelry business. In the course of their investigation the IRS has uncovered a tangled web of business and personal financial deceit involving a fraudulent investment operation perpetrated on religious organizations. Murchy's trial is slated for early next year. I'm hoping to have a front row seat.

Caroline went to Los Angeles to seek out Brittney Spears hair extension guru and fell in love with a 23-year-old "pool butler" at the Beverly Hills Four Seasons hotel. She's currently living in L.A. and taking "a break" from her marriage. Her husband has hired a nanny that's 60% Mary Poppins and 40% Mrs. Doubtfire. Her six kids have never looked healthier.

Jacardia went into hiding immediately after her Dancing with the Stars performance and has yet to surface. Unfortunately her *Closet Confidential* magazine spread with the headline, "I Like it Big!" came out two days later. Her home is currently on the market as Jacardia looks to "downsize due to some bad overseas investments" her husband made. On the upside, Jacardia, like Liz, is a star on YouTube. Her dance video has surpassed Liz's with more than a million views.

Principal Parrish immediately took early retirement.

Action New reporter Kat Alex, due to her YouTube exposure, is now working in Los Angeles for TMZ.

Jacardia, Murchy, Liz and Caroline all received bills via email, sent from the principal's computer, (an easy job for Clay once he had Mr. Parrish's password) detailing the money they owe the PTA with interest. The foul foursome were given one week to pay up or the story of their theft of school funds would go public. All four met the payment deadline.

The Spring Creek PTA didn't miss a beat. A new slate of officers was voted in the week after the Fall Festival. Heather is president, Croc Mom (currently crazy eye free) is Vice President, ABC is fundraising V.P. and Nikki is membership chair. Kelly, the lone surviving board member, cheerfully agreed to remain as the treasurer.

I'm content to stay in the background and resume my role as a mild-mannered, minivan driving mom, at least for right now . . .

Coming in April 2013

Snarky in the Suburbs - Two Weeks in Texas.

Go to www.snarkyinthesuburbs.com or Snarky In the Suburbs on Facebook for more information. I also tweet @snarkynsuburbs

CPSIA information can be obtained at www.ICGtesting.com
Printed in the USA
LVOW06s1458191115

463342LV00003B/608/P